Praise for **THE F**

"Like the magician in the first story of *The Fear of Everything*, John McNally is a master of sleight of hand, leading you, you think, one way, only to take you to someplace entirely different, entirely darker. And like the very best story writers, he can make you laugh all the way to the heartbreak, the shiver of realization when you finally see that things may not be quite as they seemed. Ranging from middle school classrooms to calls late in the night, from eerie disappearances to the people only longing for some kind of connection in the masterpiece title story, all these stories find John at the very top of his game."
—Pete Fromm, *A Job You Mostly Won't Know How to Do*

"*The Fear of Everything* is everything a short story collection should be. By turns hilarious, horrifying, and heartbreaking—and sometimes all three at once— these stories illuminate the glorious strangeness of the everyday world, in which the bright afternoons of childhood turn dark as quickly as a Midwestern sky fills with storm clouds, and ordinary people turn out sometimes to be monsters and sometimes to be capable of a kindness that surprises even themselves. With razor-sharp humor, big-hearted generosity, and a dash of the absurd, John McNally unearths an America of loneliness and longing, of vanished children and missing cats and men lost in grief, some of whom, now and then, are lucky enough to be found. An absolute delight."
—Matthew Griffin, *Hide*

Praise for *GHOSTS OF CHICAGO*
A Chicagoland Indie Bestseller
Voted one of the top twenty fiction books of 2008 by readers of *The Believer*

"McNally's seemingly mild-mannered yet unreliable protagonists prove intriguing as each deals with his or her own metaphorical monsters. Far more universal than its title might suggest, *Ghosts of Chicago* is a rollicking tour through the psyches of our modern world."
—*Rain Taxi*

"The ghosts of these stories aren't just consumed by loss, they're imprisoned by it—choosing, each time, to make their lives shrines to the past rather than taking a stab at the unknown future. In a lesser writer's hands, such stories would be predictable retreads. But McNally makes us see the real tragedy: in the absence of love, embracing grief can be the next best thing."
—NPR, "Books We Love"

Praise for *TROUBLEMAKERS*
Winner of the John Simmons Short Fiction Award
Winner of the Nebraska Book Award

"*Troublemakers* is, on every page, in every sentence, simultaneously laugh-out-loud funny and absolutely heartbreaking. John McNally's work will remind you of the greatest stories you ever heard from your best friend, or your long-lost cousin, or the improbable barroom genius you end up next to at the end of the night, except they're even better: vivid and moving and eloquent and full of the kind of moral weight that reminds you what stories are for. He has things to tell, and he does so, beautifully."
—Elizabeth McCracken, *Bowlaway*

"The author has an exquisite feel for simple, everyday aches, the heartbreaking common cruelties that people swallow, dazed, barely missing a beat. As McNally's narrators—mostly uneasy sidekicks to the 'troublemakers' of the title—bear witness to and absorb the shock of neighborhood events, readers are left a bit breathless and feel as though they are right there."
—Emily Lloyd, *School Library Journal*

THE FEAR OF EVERY THING

THE FEAR OF EVERY THING

STORIES

JOHN MCNALLY

University of Louisiana at Lafayette Press

2020

http://ulpress.org
University of Louisiana at Lafayette Press
P.O. Box 43558
Lafayette, LA 70504-3558

Library of Congress Cataloging-in-Publication Data

Names: McNally, John, 1965- author.
Title: The fear of everything : stories / by John McNally.
Description: Lafayette, LA : University of Louisiana at Lafayette Press, 2020.
Identifiers: LCCN 2020004068 | ISBN 9781946160638
(paperback ; acid-free paper) | ISBN 9781946160645 (ebook)
Classification: LCC PS3563.C38813 A6 2020 | DDC 813/.54--dc23
LC record available at https://lccn.loc.gov/2020004068

Front and back cover design by Keith Rosson
Printed on acid-free paper in the United States

Other Books by John McNally

ACKNOWLEDGMENTS

Earlier versions of these short stories appeared in various journals, magazines, and anthologies. "The Magician" first appeared in the *Sun* (2014). It was reprinted in the anthology *New Stories from the Midwest, 2015*, guest-edited by Lee Martin (New American Press, 2016). "The Lawyer" appeared in *HyperText* (2018). "The Fear of Everything" appeared in the *South Carolina Review* (2018). "The Phone Call" appeared in *Shadow Show: All-New Stories in Celebration of Ray Bradbury*, edited by Sam Weller and Mort Castle (William Morrow, 2012). "The Creeping End" appeared in *Beloit Fiction Journal* (2015). "The Blueprint of Your Brain" appeared in *One Teen Story* (2014). "The Next Morning" appeared in *Booth* (online in 2019; print in 2020). "The Devil in the Details" appeared in *HyperText* (2019). "Catch and Release" appeared in *Moon City Review* (2020).

My thanks to the University of Louisiana at Lafayette, the Department of English, and the College of Liberal Arts. I have enjoyed the support and friendship of Dayana Stetco, playwright and baker extraordinaire, who chaired the English department during much of the writing of this book. Many thanks to my other Creative Writing colleagues: Sadie Hoagland, Jessica Alexander, Henk Rossouw, and Charles Richard.

My deepest gratitude to the Dr. Doris Meriwether/BORSF Professorship for providing critical support for this project.

And, finally, my thanks to Joshua Caffery, director and publisher of UL Press, and Devon Lord, managing editor, for their willingness to take a chance on this book.

This book is for my buddy Josh Capps.
Long may you run.

TABLE OF CONTENTS

THE MAGICIAN

In 1976, the year we were supposed to be learning the metric system, we fell in love with Katy Muldoon. We were in the sixth grade, and Katy sat at the front of our math class, raising her hand for every question, as though all the answers to all the problems were merely floating in front of her eyes.

We loved her when she wore a poncho, which was an exotic thing to wear in Chicago. We loved her when she came to school with her long hair chopped short like figure skater Dorothy Hamill's. We loved her when she began crying in the middle of class one day for no reason that we could see. We loved the small scar on her forehead, just above the eyebrow, from the time she had fallen off the slide in third grade, and we loved how the scar turned purple after she ran the fifty-yard dash in gym class. We loved her when she smiled at us and when she ignored us. It didn't matter what she wore or did, we loved her regardless.

We were a pitiful lot of boys that year, the year we were supposed to learn the metric system. We rode three-speed bikes and tortured bugs. We learned how to shoot milk through our noses, to peel back our eyelids and make scary faces, and to create obscene noises with our hands and armpits. We had started growing hair in places we hadn't had hair before, and we didn't know what to think of that. We drank Tang and our mothers' Tab, and we laughed like hyenas. We were not, by even the most generous definition of the word, cool, but we didn't know that, not then at least.

What we did know was that Stu Bronson *was* cool, cooler than any of us, and far more handsome, with his blue eyes and dark, curly hair. He was in love with Katy Muldoon too, maybe even more than we were in love with her, and Katy loved that Stu loved her. We saw it in the way she blushed after he whispered to her, in the way she snuck glances at him during test time, and in the way she'd reach up to touch the scar on her forehead when she spoke to him, as though she were feeling it pulse in sync with her racing heart.

"Hey, Stu," we'd say when we caught him alone. "You and Katy . . . ?" We'd let it linger, our eyebrows raised.

Stu would give us a look that asked, *me and Katy what?* But then he'd shake his head and say, "Nah."

"OK," we'd say. "Because . . . you know . . ." And again we'd let Stu fill in the blanks.

Stu would laugh and wag that pretty head of his that we hated and then walk away. He wasn't fooling us. We knew he was lying, even if we weren't sure ourselves what we were asking, even if Stu didn't know what questions he wasn't answering.

It was the year the girls were all rounded up and ushered to the gymnasium to watch a movie while us boys played air guitar and the nose harp, stopping only when the girls returned, some giggling timidly, others acting grim. They treated us differently from before—not better, not worse, just different—and when we demanded to be taken to the gymnasium to watch the same movie they had watched so that we could see for ourselves, we were told to sit down and be quiet.

Our math class met in one of the three mobile units, a trailer that had its own coat rack and restroom. While we did our conversions from feet to meters, Mr. Bilanski, our teacher, would go into the restroom and smoke a cigarette. As soon as smoke began rolling out of the vent at the top of the wall, we would nudge one another and point at it, then sneak around the room, setting the wall clock five minutes ahead or quickly jotting down answers from the teacher's edition of the textbook.

The last week of October was Career Week, when adults would come during our math period and tell us what they did for a living and describe their jobs. The first guest was Stu's father, who was an insurance salesman. He arrived carrying a briefcase and wearing a rust-colored suit, and we were happy that he wasn't good-looking. Even though we could see only the back of Katy's head, we knew that she was watching Stu's father and wondering why he wasn't handsome and then realizing that Stu would eventually lose his good looks along with most of his hair. We asked all kinds of questions we normally wouldn't have, like, "What's Stu like at home?" and "How much money do you collect if something terrible happens to Stu?"

Mr. Bilanski, who had been staring down at a ruler as though mystified by the difference between inches and centimeters, peeked up to give us a look that meant, *Go easy, boys.*

Our own parents, who were roofers and electricians and short-order cooks, didn't come to Career Week. It hadn't crossed our minds to invite them. The other guests were friends of our teachers or people with whom somebody had done business, and they arrived wearing the clothes they wore at work. Marty Roush, a Realtor, stepped inside our mobile-unit classroom wearing a gold blazer with a giant gold nameplate pinned to his chest. Bernard Dunn, owner of an auto-repair shop, wore crisp, ironed coveralls with his first name sewn onto an oval patch over his heart. We knew by how clean his clothes were that he made other people do the dirty work, and we couldn't decide whether to envy him or hate him because of that.

On Thursday, when Mr. Bilanski introduced a travel agent named Martha as his wife, we gaped at one another, swiveling in our seats—his *wife?*—until Mr. Bilanski loudly cleared his throat. And we had to admit, she wasn't half bad. She had a nice smile and pretty ankles. We were charmed by the way she walked around the room, occasionally touching the tops of our heads. "How would you like to go to Hawaii?" she asked. And, "Do you know how much a passport costs?" We gave Mr. Bilanski sly looks that said, *Good job, old man!* but he was too busy staring at that damn ruler again.

•

When we showed up at school on Friday morning, the last day of Career Week, it was dark outside. The sky churned overhead, the wind picking up with such force that several boys' hats flew off. A younger kid whose baseball cap floated onto the grade school roof started to cry until Katy walked up to him and put her arms around him. The boy buried his head into her belly while we stood on the blacktop, watching a scene take place that we had imagined many times alone at night, except that it was *our* heads pressed against Katy's belly and *our* shoulders she had wrapped her arms around. We didn't know who the crying boy was, but we hated him now. We couldn't help it. We had come to understand that love was a daily sucker punch, and just when we thought we were over her and she didn't matter to us anymore, we'd see a boy we didn't know pressing his head against her belly and we'd feel pain in the pits of our stomachs and want to go home and pop the heads off our sisters' dolls or flush our Hot Wheels down the toilet or carry all our underwear outside and set the pile on fire while staring morosely into the flames. But more than anything else, we wanted to crawl into bed, curl up, and whisper Katy Muldoon's name, longing for what we couldn't have, until we fell asleep.

But we couldn't go home, and we couldn't crawl into bed, because it was Friday and the day had only begun. We'd been told that today's visitor was a projectionist at the local movie theater, and normally we would have been interested in what he had to say, but since we had already heard so many others talk, we wanted him to come and go as quickly as possible so that we could get back to our normal lives.

When the door opened and we saw our guest, we all took a deep breath. The man had a black mustache and goatee, and he wore black makeup around his eyes, which made them stand out the way a villain's eyes did in the old silent movies we'd seen on TV. He wore a black stove-pipe hat and a black shirt with a black cape buttoned around his neck. His pants and shoes were black as well, and he carried a black case.

"Hello, hello, hello!" he said. "I'm zee magician!" He sounded foreign, but we couldn't tell what country he was from. France? Poland? Romania?

Mr. Bilanski dropped his ruler and stood up from his desk. "Uh, I think there's been a mistake," he said.

"No mistake," the magician said. "Just . . . *magic!*" He widened his eyes, and we smiled. We liked this guy.

Mr. Bilanski seemed irritated. He disliked changes in plans, as when Mr. Delgado, our principal, spoke to him over the intercom, ordering him to bring the class to an assembly in the gymnasium. He stared at the magician for a moment. "OK, then," Mr. Bilanski said, sitting. "Come on in."

The magician shut the door behind him, and as he walked to the front of the room, he pulled coins from our ears. When he passed Katy, he pulled from her ear a small white dove. He let the bird go, and it flew to the corner and perched on top of the intercom speaker. Katy gasped, put her hands to her chest, and exclaimed that she had never seen anything so wonderful.

"Messieurs and Fräuleins," the magician said. He set his black case onto Mr. Bilanski's desk, opened it, and removed a crushed top hat that he popped into shape with his fist. "Might I have a volunteer?" he asked. Our arms shot up, but the magician looked only at Katy. "Aha!" he said. "Only one volunteer in this entire room?" Ignoring the rest of us, he held out his hand to Katy. "Up, up!" he said to her as we groaned and put our arms down. Then he turned to us and said, "My lovely—how do you say?—assistant, yes?"

We glanced over at Stu, who had crossed his arms and was frowning. We were pleased to see him looking even more dejected than we were.

Katy stood at the front of the class, holding the top hat, out of which the magician pulled a stuffed anaconda, a rotary telephone, and a bunny. He set the bunny on the floor, and it hopped across the room. The dove, still perched on the speaker, cooed. Then the magician made a magic wand levitate with one hand while quarters appeared and disappeared from between the fingers of his other hand. As he performed these feats, he asked Katy, "Are there any strings?" to which Katy yelled, "No!"

"Is there anything fishy that you can see?" he asked, and Katy, staring beyond us as though in a deep trance, yelled, "No, nothing fishy!"

When he was done, the magician stuffed the wand into Katy's ear, making it disappear, and then deposited coin after coin into that dark whorl into which we had all wished one day to whisper, "I love you, Katy Muldoon."

We applauded.

"And for my final trick," the magician said, "I would like for my lovely assistant to step inside this closet." He pointed to the restroom. We started to correct him, but the magician held up one hand to keep us quiet while he opened the door for Katy. She obeyed, waving goodbye to us before ducking inside. The magician shut the door, pulled a wand from his cape, and swished it through the air a few times. Smoke seeped from the vent at the top of the wall, the way it did whenever Mr. Bilanski went in there for a cigarette break.

The magician said, "Is this normal? Zee smoke?"

Our hearts sped up. *No*, we yelled, *it wasn't normal!*

The magician's makeup accentuated his wide eyes. "Should I check on my lovely assistant?"

Yes, we yelled, *hurry!*

When the magician opened the door, he took a step back and said, "She's gone!"

Mr. Bilanski stood from his desk, walked over to the magician, and peered inside. "What the . . . ?"

From where we sat, we couldn't see the restroom. For all we knew, Mr. Bilanski was in on the act, but there was something about both his and the magician's demeanor that made us nervous.

"*Pardonnez-moi*," the magician said, "but I must investigate." He walked into the restroom, shutting the door behind him. As soon as smoke rolled from the vent, we knew for certain it was a trick, and we expected the magician and Katy to appear from another doorway, or maybe we would see both of them watching us with amusement from a window. More smoke filled the room, causing us to cough. A shy girl named Tammy opened two windows. Mr. Bilanski scratched his chin and looked at the restroom door, then cautiously opened it and peered inside.

"It's empty," he said.

Stu joined Mr. Bilanski at the restroom. When Stu stepped inside, we considered shutting the door so that he, too, would turn into smoke, but we didn't. We just sat there waiting for Katy and the magician to return, as we knew they surely would.

Five minutes went by. Then ten. The dove remained perched on the speaker, while the bunny hopped from one end of the room to the other.

Mr. Bilanski said, "Where *is* she?" He couldn't begin the math lesson without her, but he couldn't keep waiting for her either. "Something's not right." He pushed the buzzer on the wall to call the principal's office.

Mr. Delgado was a large man with thick black hair, who reminded us of Clark Kent. He always called us "mister": "How are you today, Mr. O'Reilly? And what about you, Mr. Haleem?" But today he said, "What is it, Donald? Is there a problem?" as though we weren't even in the room.

Mr. Bilanski told him about the magician. When he described what the man had looked like, we realized that we should never have let him into the classroom in the first place.

After Mr. Bilanski finished talking to Principal Delgado, he said to us, "Wait here. I mean it. Don't leave your desks." Mr. Bilanski hurried outside, leaving the door wide open. The wind, which had been picking up all morning, caused the metal door to bang against the trailer's metal siding. It slammed repeatedly, and someone shouted, "Make sure the bunny doesn't leave!"

We noticed Stu sitting alone, across from Katy's empty seat. He was shivering. We wanted to ask him if he was OK, but we didn't. We had decided that maybe he was, in some remote way, to blame for Katy's disappearance. If Stu hadn't invited his father to Career Week, the lineup of guests would have been different, and maybe the magician wouldn't have come at all. We worked it out in our heads, making the most illogical sequence of events appear logical, and even though deep down we knew we were wrong, we weren't going to give Stu the benefit of the doubt. We needed to believe it was Stu's fault because there was no one else in the room to blame except ourselves.

•

The police spent hours interviewing us at school, asking if we had ever seen the magician before, if we knew something about Katy we hadn't told anyone, and if we were hiding anything important.

As it turned out, no one had ever seen the magician before. No projectionist in the area fit the magician's description. It complicated matters that the magician had probably dyed his hair and eyebrows and that his mustache and goatee were almost certainly fake. The police checked costume shops, interviewed local magicians, and questioned kids at other schools, but no one could say who he was.

Days turned into weeks, weeks into months, and our parents barely mentioned it except to say, "That poor girl," whenever Katy's name came up. We, on the other hand, became haunted and obsessed, meeting on the blacktop before school, huddling in the cafeteria during lunch, walking slowly home after the last bell rang, all the while going over what we knew and didn't know.

Mr. Bilanski stopped teaching us the metric system. He had begun feeding the dove and the bunny, showing up early each morning to clean up after them with the janitor's broom and dustpan. Most days he let us sleep or read our copies of *Mad* magazine. On the rare occasion that he actually taught us, he went over basic pre-algebra, things we'd already learned. But one day instead of asking, "What is x?" he tapped his chalk on the board and said, "Who is x?"

When he caught his mistake, he rubbed his eyes. "Sorry," he said, and then he pulled his pack of cigarettes from his shirt pocket, shook one out, and lit it in front of us. He hadn't gone back into the restroom since Katy had disappeared—none of us had—but this was the first time he'd smoked in our presence. He sat down, his eyes red and watery, and blew smoke toward the ceiling.

Stu lost weight. His face became gaunt, and he quit combing his hair. There were days he didn't look like he'd bathed. He furiously chewed his fingernails. We probably should have asked him how he was holding up, but we didn't. We were eleven and twelve years old, and we took pleasure in Stu's reversal of fortune even though we mourned the same loss.

•

When Principal Delgado announced that this year's talent show would be dedicated to Katy, we excitedly dove into our preparations. We were going to do stand-up comedy and gymnastics. We wrote songs and memorized lines from Shakespeare. We gathered in apartments and basements, rehearsing for hours on end, giving each other critiques. "More energy!" we'd say, or, "Not so fast!" or, "Sing like you mean it!" We had a show to put on, and by God it was going to be the best damn show anyone in our town had ever seen. And maybe—who knew?—Katy might appear at the back of the auditorium, applauding us when it was all over.

On the day of the show, two of us stayed home with the stomach flu. Others of us had practiced singing so much that our voices gave out on stage. We saw Katy's parents, Jim and Helen Muldoon, in the audience, and they forced smiles and clapped after each act, but during the performances they held hands and whispered to one another. Once, Helen Muldoon leaned her head on Jim's shoulder, and Jim began to weep—or so someone reported to us later.

After we had each failed to achieve the huge heights we were reaching for, Stu Bronson took the stage, and everyone gasped.

Stu was dressed like the magician, with a black hat and cape, a fake mustache and goatee, and black makeup around his eyes. We couldn't believe it! A few girls in the audience began to cry. The Muldoons stood up and left. Mr. P., the gym teacher, moved closer to the stage, looking as though he might climb the steps and do bodily harm to Stu, but then Stu pulled silk scarves from his mouth, one after the other, and Mr. P. stopped to watch. He made an entire deck of cards vanish. We couldn't fathom why he was doing what he was doing, but nobody would interfere. He kept making stuff appear and disappear, some things small, like foam balls, and some large, like an umbrella.

"And now," he yelled from the stage, "for my grand finale, I will bring back Katy Muldoon!"

"That's it," we heard Mr. P. say, but Principal Delgado held up his palm and told the gym teacher to wait a minute. It was as though Principal Delgado thought Stu might actually be able to do it. And we had to admit, we all thought it might happen, the reappearance of Katy Muldoon. If anyone could bring her back, we reasoned, it would be Stu Bronson, the only boy Katy had ever truly loved.

Stu made a big show of drawing shut the black velvet stage curtains behind him. Once the dark backdrop was in place, Stu waved his wand.

He chanted what sounded like a made-up spell, and then he opened the curtains. We waited. "Behold!" Stu shouted as he revealed a few feet of brick wall.

We leaned forward and squinted, but Katy was nowhere to be seen. Our hope was crushed.

Principal Delgado climbed the stage and ushered Stu away. Without any closing remarks or an announcement about who had won, the lights came up, and the talent show was over. Even though no one said it aloud, we understood that we would never see Katy again.

•

The next day at school, we knew what we were going to do. We didn't even have to talk about it.

After the final bell, we walked across the street, stopping just beyond the view of the teachers, and waited until we saw Stu Bronson. He came over to our side of the road and gave us a casual nod, as though we were all good friends. We returned the nod, out of politeness. Then we jumped him. We knocked him down, kicking and punching. Someone grabbed a hank of his hair and pulled. We expected him to scream or beg us to stop, but he lay there in silence. He winced, of course, and put his arms up to block the blows, but he did all this without making a sound, as though he had been expecting our attack, as though his performance at the talent show had been a calculated prelude to what we were doing to him now.

A few teachers stood across the street watching. Normally, teachers came over to break up fights, but today they didn't bother. Mr. Lipinski lit a cigarette and tossed the match into the street before heading to his car.

When it became clear that Stu wasn't going to fight back or cry out for help, we backed off. He remained on the ground, curled up.

"You shouldn't have done that," we said. "What were you thinking?"

Stu said nothing. He was shaking, and his nose was bleeding. The remaining teachers wandered away.

"What happened to her?" Stu finally asked, and we shrugged. "I loved Katy," Stu said, and we told him that we did, too.

When Stu covered both eyes with his fingers and sniveled, we saw that he was really just one of us. We couldn't leave Stu there, so we helped him up and brushed him off. Someone gave him a handkerchief, and then we all walked home together, dropping off one by one, until none of us were left.

•

We thought about Katy Muldoon every day for many years, and then we thought about her less, until we rarely thought about her at all. We were grown men with wives and children and divorces and secrets we kept to ourselves. We thought we had come so far from the bad manners of childhood and the ill-fitting clothes, from the shyness that overwhelmed us when a girl we liked caught our eye, from the unexpected waves of sadness and anger that we didn't know what to do with. But we were fooling ourselves. The boys were still here, and always would be.

Over the intervening years, whenever we saw a young girl with a short haircut, our hearts would inexplicably speed up, and we would think of Katy Muldoon, even though decades had passed. The magician was never heard from again. It was as though he, too, had vanished from this world, although we knew better. He was out there somewhere.

In our dreams we occasionally see both of them with perfect clarity. We are sitting in an audience, watching Katy climb into a wooden box and crouch down inside. The magician closes the hinged lid and inserts three swords into the cube: one through the side, one through the front, and one through the top. The box is on a table with caster wheels, and he spins the table around for us to see each side, and then he removes the swords. The top panel flips open, and rising up out of the box is Katy Muldoon as she would be today, a forty-eight-year-old woman. She smiles and takes a bow, having performed the greatest illusion we've ever seen, which makes us love her now more than ever, even though she has broken our hearts over and over again and will doubtless break them many more times before the magician concludes his show.

THE LAWYER

I

It had taken me two weeks to find an attorney who had earned a law degree from a university that wasn't a Bible college, an attorney who had gone to a university I had heard of—a respected university. Such an attorney was recommended to me by a law student—a guy I had once dated—who had asked around on my behalf, and according to his contacts, Taylor Lewis was the best attorney for my needs.

"He's the one, Karen," the old boyfriend texted. After I thanked him, I received another text: "Do you miss me?" When I didn't respond within the hour, he sent a sad-faced emoji. I countered with the exact same sad-faced emoji to let him know that, yes, life was indeed sad. A few minutes later, I wrote, "I'm sorry."

My needs were, on the surface, simple. I had gotten a speeding ticket. But the case became more complicated when I wrote a letter to the district attorney's office disputing the ticket since I hadn't been speeding. At all. In fact, I had just turned onto the street when a cop rounded the corner and claimed to have clocked me doing sixty-eight in a forty-five. In my letter, I asked for a list of evidence. I had found this list on a website that explained how to dispute a speeding ticket. This was not, as it turned out, a letter I should have written. I should have paid the fine. But I didn't.

My letter was passed down to the assistant district attorney, who, I discovered, had made a career prosecuting murder cases, successfully securing the death penalty. He wrote back to me that the officer, according to his notes, had given me a break, knocking the amount I had been speeding down by ten miles per hour but that he was now going to bump the speed back up to what I had been originally clocked doing, the potential penalty for which was jail time, a fine, and revocation of my license.

"You'll find attached the new court date," he concluded.

I agreed to meet the attorney, Mr. Lewis, at the Bagel Xpress for a courtesy consultation over lunch. It wasn't until I was in the parking lot that I googled Mr. Lewis and saw that his specialization was representing corporations that tested their products on animals. Had the old boyfriend misread the text about the speeding ticket? Was this his revenge for my breaking up with him? He had cried when I'd delivered the news, and it was at that moment, watching his eyes water and his lip quiver, that I knew I had made the right decision. I had hoped, three years later, that he would have gotten over it.

It was too late to cancel the appointment with the lawyer. Furthermore, I still needed representation. I locked my car and headed for Bagel Xpress, where Mr. Lewis was already halfway through his blueberry bagel, his face bright and fresh from his steaming cup of coffee.

"Hello," I said.

He set down his bagel and smiled. "Ms. Hayes," he said. "Pleased to meet you."

II

"So, what kind of bagel did you get? Looks like cinnamon sugar? Good, good. Excellent. Superb. You grow up here? No? I grew up here. Hometown boy. Went away to college. Long time ago. Went to Woodstock. *That's* how long ago. Huge Jimi Hendrix fan. Huge. I had long hair back then, too. I know, I know. Hard to believe. Smoked pot. Did I say that too loud? May have done some other things, too. Things I shouldn't say in public. We were the love generation. Free love. No inhibitions. No judgments. We were *not* going to be repressed like our parents. What was wrong with sex? What was wrong with making love? How's that bagel? I like the one they call the garbage bagel, too—you know, they put a little bit of everything in it. I can't help noticing you're not drinking coffee. You don't drink coffee? So, Hendrix at Woodstock. Amazing. I saw Janis Joplin at Woodstock. I mean, how lucky can a man be? Everyone's doing acid. Everyone's hooking up. You know the story. I met a girl there. She had four other boyfriends. I became her fifth. We all lived together in a barn for six months. This barn, it had mattresses. Some old blind fella rented the barn to her. Her name was Marie. There were other women there, too. Girlfriends of the boyfriends. Oh, man, I can't tell you how often I think about those days. Somehow—I don't remember how—we stole electricity from a pole outside. Ran an extension cord through knot-holes in the barn. Hooked up an old record player. Remember records? Good times. *Revolver* was it for us. The Beatles. And then, later, *The White Album*. But Charlie Manson ruined *The White Album* with "Helter Skelter" and murders and Sharon Tate and her beautiful unborn baby. God. An unborn baby. You don't want any butter for your bagel? Just plain? Really? Hey, whatever floats your boat. Me? I like peanut butter. Or cream cheese. Any flavor cream cheese. Doesn't matter. Anyway. Where was I? Oh, that's right. Horrible. Horrible. So after I leave the barn, I finish college and then go to law school. Chapel Hill. Good school. Solid school. And when I finish law school, what do I do? I start prosecuting child molesters. That becomes my life. This is the mid-seventies. I spend the next ten years putting child molesters in prison. If you knew what I knew about these guys . . . I mean, I don't want to go into specifics. Not here. Not in the Bagel Xpress. Not with kids around. But it's worse than you can imagine. And I took that home with me for ten years. About three years in, I had this epiphany. I was working on this case against this horrible man named Harold Jeffers. A monster, really. Had a dungeon in his nice suburban house. You want to hear the epiphany? Well, I had it because I saw in his bedroom a poster of Jimi Hendrix, and like *that*, poof, I realized that back in the sixties we were planting the seed for a

culture of predators. Our permissiveness. Our lack of a moral founda-
tion. We were sex obsessed. We thought what we were doing was okay, but
it was a sin against God. And now we're paying for it with each heinous
act committed against a child. We gave sexual predators permission, see?
Think about it. When there's a Biblical flood, the rivers rise, but when the
rain stops and the rivers begin to return to normal, another city a dozen
miles away, a city that *hadn't* flooded, will flood now because that excess
water needs somewhere to go. You can't have a generation of sexual per-
version without sexual predation down the road. As an attorney, I was
experiencing the overflowing river of a city a dozen miles away. And my
generation—perverts and sinners that we were—was to blame. You want
a different bagel? You're only nibbling at that one. They also sell hot dogs
wrapped in a kind of biscuit. Sort of like a pig in a blanket. If you're
hungry. And if you like hot dogs. I like a hot dog every now and again, but
if you eat them every day, they'll eventually kill you. Nitrates. Toenails.
Pieces of bone. But you take your chances, right? The government wants
to regulate everything. If they could, they'd regulate which side you sleep
on. If you're supposed to sleep on your left side and you accidentally roll
over to your right side in the middle of the night, you should expect a visit
from Big Government handing you a hefty fine for your infraction. I don't
know if you've noticed, but I talk a lot. But there's a point here. You know
who Roman Polanski is? Well, he's a metaphor for what went wrong. His
wife, his unborn *baby*—they were both slaughtered by the Manson family,
right? But then, what, half a dozen years later? Polanski rapes a child.
What I'm saying is this. It's cause and effect. You can't have one without
the other. I don't know if you believe in God or not. I hope you do. But
this is how God speaks to us. Not in obvious ways. He speaks to us in
consequences. People say, if there's a God, why is there war? And I say,
let me tell you stories about Roman orgies and the fall of the empire.
Speaking of stories . . . when I turned forty, I had an affair. She was an
intern in my firm. Eighteen. Nineteen. Looked up to me. Now, my story

isn't unique, right? You've heard it before. You're probably thinking, so what . . . middle-aged man has an affair with his intern. It's the most boring and obvious story in the world, right? But here's the thing. She was my best friend's daughter. Hell, I remember when she was born. I used to change her diapers when I babysat her. I probably changed her diapers a hundred times. I went to her birthday parties. My wife and I vacationed with her mother and father, and she was always with them. With us. She called me Uncle Terry. I don't know why I'm telling you all this in the Bagel Xpress, of all places. Listen, this place is gonna get crowded in about five minutes. You want one of those hot dog things? No? You sure? Okay, so I thought the affair would last a summer, but it lasted five years. And no one ever found out. Three years after it ended, my wife and I divorced. Amicably, I should add. We remain friends to this day. I remain friends with the parents of this girl I had an affair with. I make obscene amounts of money representing corporations against nutjobs like PETA. And I'm good at it. I win every case. The law is on my side. Animals don't have rights. Look, I have a dog. A pug named Cassidy. And I love that dog. But my dog isn't a person. Can we agree on that? That a dog is not a person? I don't buy sweaters for my dog, either, or dress him up in Halloween costumes. My point is this. There have been no consequences for my actions. If anything, I've been rewarded. After the affair ended, my business thrived. I've won awards from the bar association. I've been on the cover of two professional trade journals. I've told this story to a hundred clients, and still there have been no repercussions. And there's only one logical conclusion. Are you ready for this? God is rewarding me for all the good work I did putting child molesters in prison. I already paid my dues. I prevented countless other molestations. So what does God do? He offers me a taste of the forbidden fruit at no charge. He offers me my best friend's daughter. He offers me money. He, not Satan, is the snake, and the Tree of Knowledge is my law firm. What I taste in my mouth isn't sulfur. What I taste is flesh."

Mr. Lewis reaches over and takes hold of my hand. His grip is firm.

He says, "You've eaten only half your bagel, Ms. Hayes. Didn't you like it?" He lets go of my hand only after I try pulling it away. He's not looking anywhere else except in my eyes. He says, "I guess this is the point where I tell you my fees, you gasp, and then I assure you I'm a bargain because I'll wind the clock back to the moment you got your ticket. That's the best we can hope for here. But no jail time. No points against your insurance. You keep your driver's license, and what do I do? I wind the clock back to when the world was a sweeter, better place."

III

As I crossed the parking lot, a young woman walked toward me, her eyes on the Bagel Xpress sign. She was eighteen or nineteen. She looked down from the sign, saw me, stopped walking, and said, "Are you okay?"

I couldn't put in words what I was feeling, so I said, "He's waiting for you."

"Who?"

"Mr. Lewis."

She furrowed her brow. I could tell I was making her nervous. When I stepped toward her, she flinched.

"Don't go," I said. "Hire someone else."

"It's too late," she said. "My father already hired him."

"Be careful then," I said.

That night, unable to sleep, I got dressed and walked to my car. I'd heard stories of people who drove in their sleep, but this was not my case. I was wide awake.

I lived next to a two-lane highway, the one on which I had been accused of speeding. The highway had once cut through farmland but now sliced through housing developments where only three different styles of houses sat on small plots with newly planted trees. I had never driven to where the new houses ended and the farmland resumed, but tonight I was determined to do just that.

The speed limit was forty-five, but I drove fifty-five, sixty-five, and then seventy-five. Fifteen miles from home, a police car fired up its lights and fell in behind me. Ten miles later, two more squad cars joined the chase. I pushed on the accelerator, inching up to a hundred. I saw barns ahead, one on either side of the road. One was still sturdy, the other imploding in on itself. There was a hole in its roof, as though an asteroid had hit it. There were no other sounds in the night except for the roaring sirens. In my peripheral vision, illuminated by the high beams, I saw squirrels and rabbits, a stray dog. A gang of deer stood off to the side of the road, all of them frozen in place. I have spoken to the devil, I thought. I imagined looking into my rearview mirror and seeing a constellation of glowing eyes, a thousand animals oblivious to the horrors that lie ahead, but when I finally glanced up, I saw only red and blue swirling lights— and the blurred faces of men hunting me down.

THE FEAR OF EVERYTHING

Larry needed to purge. He needed to reinvent himself so that people would stop looking at him with pity. He was still young—fifty-two. There was plenty of time for a detour. Until now, everyone saw Larry as a guy who was nothing if not rock steady: clear-eyed, not particularly driven but not lazy, a solid B-minus of a man. But he wanted to up his game, turn himself into a person that no one would have expected, and so one overcast Sunday afternoon he boxed up all his and Sarah's clothes and drove it to Goodwill.

What a relief to walk into his empty bedroom. It was as though the closets, glowing now from virgin light, were themselves taking in deep breaths. Gone was the vintage sweatshirt with Snoopy and Woodstock. Gone was the pink Izod polo shirt that never fit quite right. Gone, along with everything else that had belonged to her, was Sarah's wedding dress. Every belt, every scarf, every reminder of his life before today: gone, gone, gone.

He quit his job as vice president at Southeast Savings and Loan and became a manager at the last Family Video in town. He bought a Mustang V6 convertible. He grew a handlebar mustache that he could twirl at the ends. He shaved his head. In honor of an old Jim Croce song, he got a tattoo on one arm that said, "Baby," and a tattoo on his other arm that just said, "Hey." He quit eating meat; he quit drinking coffee. When friends asked him how he was holding up, he said, "Really well," and when they didn't look convinced, he'd add "No, really," before shuffling them along to the next subject, all the while aware that they were staring at his mustache, his bald gleaming dome, and his fresh tattoos.

In his previous life, he would never have chatted up a waiter or waitress taking his order, but now he asked about the daily specials, he commented on the uniqueness of their names if their names were indeed unique, and he asked for recommendations for things to do in town, as though he were a weary traveler who had serendipitously found himself in a mysterious place for the night, ready to lift the lid of this town's treasure chest to see what jewels it had to offer him.

One night, a waitress named Kelly asked him if he was a musician, and instead of telling her about his new job at the video store, he said, "Yes. Jazz fusion. I play the flute."

"The flute!" she said, smiling as he suspected she would.

"I'm a flutist," he said, smiling back at her. "Is there a problem with that?"

"No," she said, holding back a laugh. "No problem at all."

They were flirting, he and Kelly, and (after several drinks at the restaurant bar after she got off work) they ended up back at her place, where six cats roamed her apartment, occasionally confronting one another with hisses and swipes, like a pack of lonely bar-goers who've been sent out into the night after last call. She had an AeroBed, and in the three minutes it took to inflate with the electric pump, she told him the names of her cats between kissing him on the mouth, a kiss for each name: Miles and Duke and Ella and Billie and Dizzy and Bird.

"So you know about jazz," he whispered into her mouth, and she replied, "A little."

In the morning, Kelly said, "How's my favorite flautist?" and Larry thought, *So this is how my new life's going to be.* And he wasn't altogether unhappy about it.

•

Larry had quit mowing his lawn. He let the grass grow, the weeds take over. The garden, which had been home to a hundred different genera of plants, went neglected.

His neighbor, Mufeed Abdullah, walked up Larry's driveway one afternoon when Larry was about to get into his Mustang. Mufeed was not a subtle man. He eyed the yard for a good, long while before turning his gaze on Larry.

"The grieving process is a long one, yes?" Mufeed said.

Larry shrugged then nodded.

"Hey, baby," Mufeed said.

Larry cocked his head before realizing that Mufeed was reading his tattoos. "Jim Croce?" Larry said. "Singer-songwriter? Died in a plane crash in Louisiana?"

Mufeed made a noise that could have been approval or disapproval, sympathy or annoyance. His face was as lumpy and as impassive as a cantaloupe. He said, "My cousin does yards. If you like, I can give you his number. He, too, has a bald head and a funny mustache."

"I'm fine," Larry said. "For now. But thank you."

Mufeed smiled, but it wasn't a smile, not really. It was his way of saying, *Okay then . . . the conversation is over.* Larry returned the nonsmile smile, then quickly backed out of his driveway and sped away.

At night, after work, Larry toiled away on OkCupid. The dating site had questions that you could answer or not answer, thousands of them. The more you answered, the more accurate your match percentage. For most of the questions, there were no wrong or right answers, but a few of the questions were indeed fact based. For instance: *Which is larger, Earth or the sun?* Women who answered "the Earth" tended to be low percentage matches for Larry. 21 percent. 18 percent. They also tended to be diametrically opposed to Larry's positions on ethics, religion, and dating. And yet they were the ones who most often liked Larry's profile. It was as though evidence of their incompatibility were an aphrodisiac. Why couldn't they see that Larry was their absolute worst choice?

In an attempt to attract a kind of woman who normally wouldn't have been attracted to Larry but who fit his agenda—his agenda being to mutate into a Larry who would be unrecognizable to his family and friends—he answered hundreds of sex questions not always based on his own true feelings or predilections but based instead on his desire to manipulate the algorithm to his liking. Therefore, when asked if he would squeal like a dolphin during sex if his lover asked him to, he answered yes. Would you prefer to be tied down or do the tying? Do the tying. Would he let a lover pee on him? Sure, why not. Was it okay for a spouse to fool around with the other spouse's consent? Of course. How open are you to trying new things in bed?

Larry's eyes pulsed from having answered over two thousand questions in total. He lay in bed, his phone close to his face. He clicked "A"—"Very open. I'll try anything once"—and then put his phone on the bedside table and fell into a sleep of two-fisted dreams where the sun belched its last gaseous ray and Earth, around which everything circled, turned as icy as the rink around which Larry and Sarah had once skated when they were children and not yet in love.

•

The message was waiting for him when he woke up. It was from a woman named Zoe. The message was long, specific, inviting. It began, "I really enjoyed reading your profile," continued with observations of their shared likes, including movies by Kurosawa and songs by Tom Waits, and ended with, "If you are interested in meeting me and my husband for a possible playdate, please let me know ASAP."

Larry studied her photos. In each one, her hair was a different color: blue or red or purple or green; and she was covered with tattoos of vines and vampires and the faces of movie stars who had died tragically, like Jayne Mansfield and Marilyn Monroe. Her husband appeared in a few photos wearing a cabbie hat and a full beard. His eyebrows were especially thick. To his credit, he had good teeth and an engaging smile.

A playdate, Larry thought. What would his friends and family think about *that?*

In his response, Larry hit all the right notes, waiting several sentences to confirm his interest in a playdate only after he'd had a few meaningful but pithy things to say about *Seven Samurai* and *Mule Variations*. And then, yes, by all means, let's set up a date for the three of us to meet! In your photos, he added, you remind me of a young Patricia Arquette. 1992. 1993. *True Romance*, he concluded before hitting send and then immediately wishing he could go back to edit, remembering the horrible, violent things that had happened to Patricia Arquette's character in *True Romance*. But it was too late.

•

The hedges on either side of Larry's sidewalk, untrimmed and almost touching, like the fingers of Adam and God in an endless and surreal foliage version of Michelangelo's *The Creation of Adam*, obscured the presence of Mufeed until Larry was almost on top of him. Behind Mufeed stood a short, squat man wearing dirty clothes. His head was not shaved, but he was bald, with a rim of hair remaining, and he had a very particular goatee that made him look vaguely like a short, squat Frank Zappa. He held his hand out toward Larry, and Larry shook it. He introduced himself as Mufeed's cousin, Ghassan. Where Mufeed still had the hint of an accent from the old country, Ghassan sounded like a carnival barker.

"Mufeed says you need some yard work done," Ghassan said. "You got poison oak all over the place. So, get this. I'm not allergic. I'm like a goat. I can eat that shit all day, and I'd be fine. Howzabout I give you an estimate, buddy? You got a lot of real estate here. Oh, and I'm sorry for your loss. Truly." He shook his head, as though miming grief, then reached up and felt the weight of the overgrown shrubbery with his palm.

Larry said, "I appreciate it, Ghassan. But I'll get around to it. I'm just on a different schedule these days. My internal clock isn't the same as it used to be."

Mufeed said, "I don't believe in internal clocks."

Ghassan, pointing to Mufeed, said, "This guy. Always so serious."

Larry said, "Gentlemen?" And then he headed for his Mustang.

All day at work, he received messages from Zoe, and he promptly answered them. Her messages came so fast, he became an almost entirely internal being, thinking only of her, what little he knew, the images of her, and the anticipation of her next message. Normally at work, he remained in the trenches with his employees—helping customers, shelving DVDs, answering the phone—but today he was distracted, and his employees saw it. Jeremy, who was attending film school at the local arts college, noted that Larry had shelved *I Spit on Your Grave 2: Unrated* in the children's section, next to *How to Train Your Dragon*. "Duly noted," Larry replied before looking back into the pulsing dark heart of his cell phone.

•

They had agreed to meet that very night, Larry and Zoe and Zoe's husband, whose name Larry still did not know. It would be a casual get-to-know-you meeting at their house. "Let's see if we all like each other," Zoe wrote. She added, "We haven't done this very often. In case you were wondering. We're very choosey."

"How often?" Larry asked, and Zoe responded, "Less than a dozen, more than nine."

In what world, he wondered, was that not a lot? Perhaps it was Larry's perception that was out of whack. Just a taste of what he had read in various OkCupid profiles hinted at love lives that were far more complicated and much richer than anything he had ever imagined. While Larry didn't in any way regret the life he'd lived with Sarah, New Larry (as he had recently begun to think of himself) was going to embrace the multifaceted world of romance, in all its thorny configurations.

"Why, hello there, Flute Man!"

Larry looked up from a rack of T-shirts with logos of mundane name brands, like Kodak and Schwinn and Kentucky Fried Chicken. Standing before him was the waitress with the six cats. Kelly.

"Herbie Mann was a flutist," she said. Was she flirting?

"Oh yes," Larry said. "Herbie Mann. That's right." He couldn't think of anything else to say, so he said, "Two *n*'s in Mann, right?"

"Anyway," Kelly said. "I just wanted to say hello. That's all. Nothing more."

"No," Larry said. "Thank you. I'm glad you did."

"Hey, baby," she said, and Larry, feeling for the first time self-conscious about his choice of tattoos, said, "Exactly." And then Kelly walked away.

•

Zoe and Zoe's husband lived in a nice bungalow on a street lined with old magnolia trees.

Larry was heading up to Zoe's front door when he noticed a concrete Loch Ness Monster in their yard, the kind of thing you'd buy in *Sky* magazine. He knocked on Zoe's door, waited, and then knocked again.

Zoe's husband—or, at least, the man in the photos—opened the front door. The sight of this man made Larry anxious since he had gotten into his head that Zoe, and not her husband, would be the first to greet him. In fact, he had convinced himself that her husband wouldn't be home at all, not at first; that he and Zoe would have a chance to get to know each other—to chat—before the husband would even be introduced. And now here the man was, more heavily bearded and eyebrowed than in his photos.

"I'm Zoe's husband," he said, shaking Larry's hand. With this, he stepped out of the house. Keeping his voice low, he said, "We've got a bit of a problem. I don't know if Zoe has told you this, but she suffers from pantophobia."

"No," Larry said. "She hasn't. She didn't." He hesitated. Then: "What's pantophobia?"

"It's the fear of everything," he said.

"Really!" Larry said. "The fear of everything?"

Zoe's husband nodded. He said, "Dig the shirt."

"What?"

"KFC."

"Oh yeah. It's new." Larry had forgotten that he was wearing his shirt with the Kentucky Fried Chicken logo.

"Cool," Zoe's husband said, and then he carefully considered his next words before speaking. "Some days," he began. "Some days are better than other days. Today? Not so good, man."

"Shit," Larry said. "I'm sorry." And then: "The fear of *everything*?"

Zoe's husband nodded. He said, "We need to reschedule. I'm sorry, dude. She's said good things about you." He looked down at Larry's arms and said, "I like your ink, man."

"Thank you."

They shook hands again, and Larry headed back to his Mustang. Inside his car, he checked his messages, and there was one from Zoe that said, simply, "I'm really sorry. Some days, it's bad. But other days, I can't even leave my bedroom. The worse it gets, the smaller my world becomes. The anxiety is crushing. I'm really sorry. I'm really, really sorry."

"It's okay," Larry wrote back. "We'll try again another time. I promise."

But a month went by without a word from Zoe. Then two months went by. Larry stopped at the restaurant with the hope of running into Kelly, but a waiter told him that she had moved to Pensacola with a man she'd met at the restaurant. Furthermore, and much to their delight, everyone who worked at the restaurant now owned one of her cats.

"Was he a flutist?" Larry asked, smiling, but the waiter merely looked confused.

"No," he said. "He was a tool and die maker. But he had a mustache like yours."

"Oh, really," Larry said, and asked for a to-go box for his leftovers.

He passed his days at work googling all the articles he could find about pantophobia, described as the insistent dread of some unidentified evil. It was possible that the word pantophobia was related to Pan, the Greek god of mountain wilds and rustic music, companion to the nymphs. Larry had read that Pan could multiply into a swarm of Pans, each with his own name and his own life separate from the original Pan. It seemed a miraculous thing, like the division of a cell, which he only vaguely remembered from high school biology. But it also seemed like the premise of a horror movie, the kind he might have stocked in the cult movie section of the video store.

Larry stood behind the counter and ate ice cream bars without paying for them. He wore his Kentucky Fried Chicken T-shirt and told customers that they didn't carry movies that they did carry, like *Star Wars* and *Goodfellas*. One night, an old friend of Sarah's came in to rent a movie. Her name was Lucy, and she had been to their house no fewer than a hundred times over the twenty-five years that he and Sarah were married, and Larry knew some of the most personal details about Lucy's life, like how she'd had all her toenails removed because of a fungus she couldn't eradicate. Lucy and Sarah had had a falling out four years ago, and Larry hadn't seen her since. When she brought her movie to the checkout, she looked up and gasped.

"Larry?" she said.

"I know, I know," he said. "It's a new look."

"No, that's not it," Lucy said.

"What is it then?" Larry asked.

Lucy said, "I thought you were dead."

Larry smiled, laughed nervously. "I'm sorry?" he asked.

"I heard what happened, and . . ." She paused. She shook her head. "I'm sorry. It's good to see you, Larry."

"Good to see you, too, Lucy," Larry said, although he didn't mean it. Not now.

She paid with a VISA, thanked Larry, then collected the movie from him on the other side of the security gate. As he watched her drive away, he felt a pang of remorse along with something else he couldn't put his finger on, but it was a feeling he suspected people felt when they stepped out of their storm cellar and saw that their entire neighborhood had been sucked up by a tornado, twirled several dozen times, and let go.

"Hey, baby," a man said, and Larry looked up to see Zoe's husband nodding toward his tattoos. "Larry, right?" he asked.

Larry, still clueless of the man's name, said, "Yes. And you're . . . ?"

"Zoe's husband," Zoe's husband said.

"Of course," Larry said. "Yes." After a pause, Larry said, "How is she? Zoe?"

"You haven't heard?"

"No." His heart pounded. What hadn't he heard?

Zoe's husband said, "Oh. We're separated."

"Really?"

"Word," Zoe's husband said. "I figured she'd have told you."

"I haven't heard anything from her since that night."

"Oh. Yeah. Well. She gets like that." He sighed. "Pantophobia is a bitch. No shit."

"I can imagine," Larry said.

"No," Zoe's husband said. "You can't imagine." He took a deep breath then sighed. "No offense."

"None taken."

After Zoe's husband left, Larry sent Zoe a message, saying he had run into her husband and heard the news and that he was very sorry. Please let me know if there's anything I can do, he wrote. Anything at all.

•

That night, Larry was jarred awake to what sounded like a helicopter circling his house. He remembered one year ago regaining consciousness to the same sound, but why was there a helicopter hovering near his bedroom window tonight?

Larry got out of bed, parted the curtains, and looked outside. It wasn't a helicopter. It was Mufeed's cousin, Ghassan, driving a large riding lawnmower with a high-powered headlight, cutting through weeds as high as cornstalks. No doubt Mufeed had given Ghassan the go-ahead to take care of the yard.

Unable to sleep, Larry logged onto OkCupid, and for the first time in months, there was a message from Zoe. It read simply, "I need your help. The key is under the first hump of the fake Loch Ness Monster in the front yard."

Wearing sweatpants and his Kentucky Fried Chicken T-shirt, he drove to Zoe's. In Zoe's front yard, he lifted the first cement hump, which weighed more than he'd anticipated, causing his back to spasm. Inside a plastic-snap case was the key, damp and rusting. Only after inserting the key and turning the lock did he wonder if he was being set up. After all, he'd never even met Zoe. What if he was being catfished? What if Zoe was really just a creation of Zoe's husband? And what if it was Zoe's husband and not Zoe waiting for him?

The house was dark. Larry shut the door behind him. A small animal, possibly a cat, ran by, and he thought about the night he pretended to be a flutist and how he'd spent his night on an air mattress with a woman he'd just met while shadows of cats stretched across the walls and ceiling, looming as large as cheetahs and tigers. His new life had seemed so promising back then, but, ever since, he had faced hurdle after hurdle, and no one, except for Zoe, had responded to New Larry with the enthusiasm he'd hoped.

"Zoe?" he called out.

"Back here," a voice returned.

Larry moved toward the voice, but he lost his direction after a few feet in the dark. "Again!" Larry yelled.

"I'm back here," Zoe said. "All the way in the back."

Larry entered a bedroom at the rear of the house. When he flipped on the light, Zoe yelled, "No! No light!" and he flipped it back off, but he had not seen her.

"Where are you?" he asked.

She didn't answer, but he could hear her breathing, possibly hyperventilating. When he walked toward a closet and opened its door, he heard the breathing unmuffled now. He couldn't see anything, but he could tell that the closet was stuffed full of clothes, and when he crouched to his knees, he felt dozens of shoes. He reached toward the breathing but touched Zoe's knee instead, and then he pushed aside a small mountain of footwear and crawled into the closet beside her.

"Shut the door," Zoe said. Larry shut the door. "It's too big in here," she said. "There's too much room."

"No, no," Larry said. "It's too small."

"I can't breathe," Zoe said.

"You're going to be fine," Larry said. "It's all right. I'm here now. I'm with you."

He put his arm around her and hugged her toward him, and she put her arms around his torso. She was shivering despite the heat.

Sitting at the back of a closet in the pitch-black, Larry eventually lost all sense of temporal and spatial orientation. He could have been anywhere in the world right now. He could have been in Japan or Belgium or, as was the case last summer, in the ditch of a small unmarked road thirty miles north of Greensboro. He could have been inside a boat or an airplane or a one-year-old Honda CR-V with four-wheel drive. With the helicopters' lights flooding the CR-V while he hung upside down, unable to unbuckle himself to help Sarah, there was nothing that he didn't fear, and the thought of what the rest of his life might be like was as unimaginable as living on a planet that was larger than the sun.

"I'll be here as long as you need me," Larry said to Zoe, "but eventually we're going to move out into the bedroom. And then into the rest of the house. And then outside."

Zoe didn't say anything at first, but then, in a tired and raspy voice, she said, "Okay."

"All right then," Larry said hopefully.

"But only when I'm ready," Zoe said.

"Of course." He tried to think of something to say. He said, "Did you know that Pan is the only Greek god to die?"

"No," Zoe said. "I didn't."

"Imagine," he said, "being the only one. Imagine how cheated you'd feel."

"I can't imagine," Zoe said.

"I know," Larry said. "Me neither."

And that was all he could think to say. Together, they listened to the city's street-cleaning vehicle with its whirring brushes. Eventually Zoe fell asleep, her head resting on his shoulder. As Larry began to drift off, tucked comfortably in that space between being awake and being asleep, he said, "She was a botanist." In his sleep, he heard an approaching buzz, a swarm of Larrys surrounded by the daughters of river gods, and for a moment he dreamed that he was a Titan, a god among mortals, instead of what he really was: a fifty-two-year-old man, lonely and frightened, with nowhere else to be.

THE PHONE CALL

Dougie had been home from the hospital only an hour when Bob, Dougie's uncle, opened the bedroom door and flipped off Dougie's light without saying a word. The door creaked shut, and footsteps grew softer as his uncle retreated.

Dougie wanted the light back on. He was six years old and couldn't sleep, his throat still pulsing from where his tonsils had been removed. In his room at the hospital he could at least turn on the TV or buzz for the nurse, with whom he had fallen in love, but here at home he had to remain in bed, and all there was to do was study his walls, which he had decorated with covers from his favorite magazine, *Famous Monsters of Filmland*. With the light out, he couldn't even do that.

Dougie had no idea what time it was. He passed the hours thinking about Nurse Jill, who had long, straight, blonde hair like Susan Dey in *The Partridge Family*, and how she had rubbed her hand over his hair and said, "I know girls who'd *kill* for those curls." She leaned close to him, almost to his mouth, and whispered, "But you probably hate them, don't you?" With her mouth so close to his own, Dougie wanted to sit up and kiss her. Instead, he stared into her foam-green eyes until she touched his nose with the tip of her finger and stood up.

Dougie replayed that particular memory over and over, because if he let it fade away it would be replaced by the man he saw right after he'd woken up from his surgery. The man lay motionless in the bed next to him—tubes running into his mouth, a machine beeping continuously, his skin the color of Silly Putty. When the doctor saw that Dougie had come to, he nodded angrily toward Nurse Jill, who swiftly pulled the curtain shut between them. Dougie, barely able to keep his eyes open, eventually fell back to sleep. The next time he woke up, he saw two men wearing white shirts and white pants rolling the man out of the room, a blanket covering all of him, including his head, the way Dougie liked to sleep with a flashlight under the covers whenever he stayed awake to look at his magazines with their photos from *Dracula* and the *Creature from the Black Lagoon*.

"What was his name?" Dougie asked Nurse Jill later that day.

Nurse Jill smiled. "Mr. Belvedere."

"Where'd he go?" Dougie asked.

Nurse Jill reached down and rested the tip of a finger inside one of Dougie's curls. Testing the curl's buoyancy, she said, "To a better place."

A better place, Dougie thought now, in his bedroom, in the dark. Over the years Doug would meet other people, strangers mostly, with remarkably similar stories, of waking up in a haze of anesthesia next to a dead person whose soul was being spirited away. *Did everyone have such stories?* he would wonder.

The phone in the hallway rang.

The ring was so loud, Dougie's heart sped up.

The phone continued to ring. Wouldn't Uncle Bob or his mother answer it? Bob was his father's brother, but Dougie didn't remember anything about his father. The man had died when Dougie was still a baby. A hunting accident, he'd been told. No, his earliest memories of any man in the house were of Uncle Bob, who came sniffing around every few days like a stray dog, often spending the night.

On the fifth ring, Dougie slid out of bed and, feeling his way from one end of his room to the other, eased open his door.

In the hallway, he could lean against the banister and see the living room below, where aquarium light sprayed gently up toward Dougie, causing the walls to look like they were alive and moving, as though he were the one inside the fish tank. He picked up the phone.

"Hello?" he whispered.

A man called out from the earpiece: "Hello? Hello? Who is this? Is this Dougie?"

Dougie did not recognize the man's voice. "Who are you?" he asked. And then a chill blew up under his pajamas, causing him to shiver. "Is this Mr. Belvedere?"

"Who's Mr. Belvedere? Tell me about him."

"He's in a better place now," Dougie said.

"He's dead?" the man asked. "Did someone kill him?"

"He's in a better place now," Dougie repeated, but he felt like weeping this time because he didn't know who this man was or why he was asking questions.

"Listen," the man said. "I don't have much time, and you won't hear from me again for another couple of years, so I want you to do something for me, okay? I want you to remember who I am. I want you to pay attention. Because something terrible is going to happen, and only you can stop it."

The harder Dougie cried, the worse his stitched and bleeding throat hurt. He began to moan from the pain.

"Don't cry, Dougie," the man said. "Don't cry. I'm your friend. You have to believe me. I'm your . . ."

Dougie hung up and returned to his bedroom, leaving behind the room with walls that looked like they were breathing and a phone call he would barely remember in a week. He could have turned on his bedroom light now, but he was afraid to. He wouldn't see those walls again until morning, when sunlight seeped through his curtains, waking all the monsters.

•

Thirty years later, Doug sits at the Tick Tock Lounge with a baker's dozen of his coworkers from Rockwell International. The three tables they had pushed together earlier in the night now harbor a collection of beer mugs and pitchers and shot glasses, glasses for highballs and martinis, peeled-off beer bottle labels and soggy napkins. Someone had slammed her beer down onto the last jalapeño popper, squeezing cheese out at both ends, causing it to look like a thick worm that's been stepped on.

Across from Doug sits Louise Malgrave, who keeps touching Doug's ankle with her toes and then acting as though it's an accident.

"Is that you again?" she asks, smiling. She reaches over and taps his hand with her fingernails. She can't *not* touch him, it would seem. "I'm sorry." Louise is a supervisor at Rockwell while Doug does data entry, typing in long strings of code that he doesn't understand.

"It's okay," Doug says. He considers asking her to go home with him—why not?—but when he leans toward her, what comes out of his mouth surprises even him: "This is the anniversary of my mother's death," he says. He forces a grim, hopeless smile and, almost as an after-thought, adds, "She was murdered when I was fifteen."

"Oh no!" Louise says, and her face droops, as if sympathy and muscle control are incompatible. She looks a dozen years older now, and whatever vague plans Doug had had with her in mind crumble before him.

What Doug has said is true—his mother *was* murdered, and today *is* the anniversary—but he can't stand the way Louise is looking at him, the pity, the anguish, so he shakes his head and says, "I'm kidding."

"What?"

"I'm drunk. I'm sorry."

"You're a jerk," Louise says. His coworkers stop talking to see why Louise is so angry. "He's a *jerk*," Louise says to her captive audience. "You know what he told me?"

"Actually," Doug says, keeping his voice low, "it's *true*. It's just that . . . I don't know . . . the way you were looking at me."

Jerry, Doug's boss, stands up from his end of the table and walks over. He's eighty pounds overweight and speaks in a voice that sounds like every businessman Doug's ever overheard: deep, loud, fake. "Hey, now," he says, smiling. "Everything okay over here?"

"Fine," Doug says, standing. Louise is crying but shrugging away those who want to comfort her, even though it's obvious she wants the attention. "It's fine," Doug continues. "A misunderstanding is all."

Jerry nods. He escorts Doug to the Tick Tock's exit, and together they stand in the glow of neon beer signs. "Let's talk on Monday, shall we?"

Doug nods. "Okay. All right." He reaches out to shake Jerry's hand, but Jerry turns and heads toward Louise Malgrave, leaving Doug with his arm outstretched.

•

Doug hits three more taverns on his way home. By the time he reaches his apartment foyer, he's having a hard time inserting the miniature key into his mailbox lock. He rests his head against the wall, shuts his eyes, and tries inserting the key one last time. This time it goes in. When he opens the door, a fat phone bill falls out onto the chipped tile floor.

"Dammit," he says when he sees it's the same phone company he's been having problems with. His long-distance phone service had been slammed. Doug had heard the term *slammed* for the first time only recently when news reports popped up about a local renegade phone company taking over people's long-distance service without the customers' approval. It's illegal, of course, but extraordinarily difficult to stop once it's set in motion. The name of this company is Blue Skies.

Doug tears open the phone bill as he mounts the stairs to his apartment, and after banging open his door and flipping on the kitchen light, he examines the bill. Amount Due: $3,456.72.

"Three thousand and *what?*" he yells. "Are they *kidding?*" He squints at the phone bill.

He walks into his bedroom, where he has hung all the old covers from the magazine *Famous Monsters of Filmland*, the same covers he'd hung on his wall in childhood. They are torn now and fading, but he can't bring himself to take them down. The thought of doing so fills him with an inexplicable sadness. He clings to his monsters, the way others cling to old blankets or favorite coffee mugs.

Doug climbs into bed with his shoes on. The heavy black rotary phone sits like a purposefully silent and endangered reptile, the last of its kind, on his bedside table. He picks up the receiver and dials the number for Blue Skies.

"Blue Skies," a woman says. "My name is Bethany. How may I help you?"

"How may you help me," Doug says coldly, staring into the eyes of Lon Chaney as Mr. Hyde. "First off, Bethany, you can tell me how it's even possible for my bill to be over three thousand dollars."

"The amount due," Bethany begins, "is based on how many calls you . . ."

Doug cuts her off. "*Look*," he yells. "I didn't even sign up with your company. What you're doing is illegal. I want you to switch me back to my old provider."

"I'm sorry," Bethany says, "but it's too late. There's nothing to be done."

"What the hell do you mean it's too late, that there's nothing to be done?"

"Sir," Bethany says. "Please lower your voice."

"I *won't* lower my voice. I . . ."

The phone goes dead.

"Hello? Bethany? Hello?"

Doug slams down the phone. He calls back and Bethany answers again.

"Are you calm now, sir?"

"Look," Doug says. He shuts his eyes. He's drunk and sleepy. He can feel the room spinning, the way the city park's merry-go-round felt when his Uncle Bob started to push it faster and faster—Dougie crying, begging him to stop because it was going too fast and he could barely hang on. He starts dreaming about that time in his life when he hears a voice in his ear: "Hello? Are you still there?"

"Who is this?" Doug asks.

"It's Bethany."

"Hi, Bethany," Doug whispers. He waits for her to say something, but when she doesn't, he asks, "What are you wearing?"

"I beg your pardon?"

"I'm in bed," Doug says. "Where are *you*?"

"Maybe *that's* why your bill is so high," Bethany says sharply. "Those sorts of calls are expensive. Now, goodnight, sir," she says and hangs up.

Doug falls asleep with the phone against his ear until he's woken by a loud beeping, a phone off its hook. He returns the phone to its cradle, stares at it for a good while, then picks up the receiver again. Every year, on the anniversary of his mother's death, he dials his old home's phone number, a number that has remained etched in his mind, even though it's been disconnected for years.

Concentrating, he puts his finger in the rotary's dial, draws his finger to the right for each number, and lets it go. He expects the familiar we're-sorry-but-you've-reached-a-number-that's-no-longer-in-service message, but a woman answers on the second ring, an actual human being, and Doug quickly sits up.

"Hello?" she says. A baby is crying in the background.

"Hello?" Doug says. "Who's this?"

"Hey, who's *this*?" the woman asks. She laughs, and a chill runs through Doug. *He knows this woman*. The baby cries louder now, and the woman is saying, "Hush, hush, Sweetie." A doorbell rings. "Hold on there," the woman says to Doug. He hears the phone getting set down; he hears footsteps, a door opening, voices. And then he hears what sounds like a hurt animal, a sound that frightens Doug, has always frightened Doug—the plaintive wailing of grief. What's happening?

"Hello!" Doug yells into the phone. "What's going on there? Hello!"

He hears someone moving toward the phone. The receiver is lifted, and a man says, "Who is this?"

"It's Doug. Who's this?"

"Doug?" The man sounds confused, disoriented. "I don't know what you're selling, Doug, but you'll have to call another time. There's been an accident here." The phone is hung up with a thud.

Doug removes the receiver from his ear and stares at it. He knows he shouldn't do this, but he dials the number again, just to confirm that he did indeed dial his old phone number. If the same man answers, he'll simply hang up. But it's the woman this time.

"Hello?" She sounds tired now. Doug hears a young child in the background calling out, "Mommy, mommy, mommy."

"Hush," the woman says sharply to the child. And then again: "Hello?"

"Hi," Doug says. "I was just calling to make sure everything is okay."

"I'm sorry?" the woman says. "I think you have the wrong number?"

It's the way she ends her sentences as questions that exhumes the past, confirming for Doug who it is he's speaking to: *his mother*. He hasn't heard her voice in over thirty years, a voice he thought he would never forget, but as one year folded into another, one decade after the other disappearing behind him, he found it harder and harder to conjure her up as she had once been. Her voice had been the first to fade, until he couldn't remember her inflections on certain words or the precise way she still carried her own southern childhood in her speech. For the first time, he experiences what everyone else who's ever stepped into his bedroom has experienced, that all the monsters on his walls are staring directly at him.

"This is Shirley, isn't it?" he asks. His own voice cracks. He's trying not to cry.

"It *is*," she says suspiciously. "And who are *you?*"

There is no way he can explain to her who he is. He can only try to keep her talking.

"We met a few years ago," he says. "I worked with your husband, Tim." Silence. "My name's Frank Ivers. You wouldn't remember me," Doug says and forces out a laugh. He hears the child in the background again. The child is him. He's listening to his younger self. "I didn't know Tim well," Doug says, "but I always liked him. I'm just calling . . ." He pauses. He's shivering but trying not to. "I'm just calling to see how you're holding up."

He hears his mother lighting a cigarette. This means she's settling in for a long conversation.

"It hasn't been an easy three years," she says. "The day Bob came home with the news . . ." She blows smoke into the mouthpiece. She's sitting down now, Doug imagines. "It was the worst day of my life."

"I'm so sorry," he says. "I just want you to know that I'm a friend."

His mother makes a noise of assent, but she's lost in her own world. How many times had he seen this, his mother sitting on the couch and staring straight ahead as he tried to get her attention, showing her the cover of his new *Famous Monsters of Filmland*?

"Something's not right," she says finally. "I can't put my finger on it, but . . ."

"Yes?"

Doug hears something rumbling in the background. A pickup truck?

"I've got to go," his mother says.

"Who is it, Shirley? Is it Bob?"

The phone goes dead.

Doug is pacing the room, two fingers holding the heavy black phone, the phone's base resting against his thigh. He sets down the phone, hangs up the receiver. After his father's death, Bob began coming over more frequently, sometimes spending the night on the couch. Doug's earliest memories are of his uncle snoring on their sofa as his mother tiptoed through the room and scolded Doug for playing too loudly with his Hot Wheels. "You don't want to wake that man" was how she put it.

Doug was fifteen when his mother was murdered. A homeless man, who had been Dumpster diving, discovered Shirley's body in a large trash bin behind an apartment complex. She was wrapped in a large blue tarp. People who lived in the apartment building had thrown leaking bags of garbage on top of her, unaware that a body was there. An autopsy revealed that she had died from severe blunt head trauma. Police had detained the homeless man as a possible suspect, but there was nothing to connect him to his mother, and no weapons of any kind had been found on him. No weapon of any kind had ever been found. Bob had been questioned, too, but he'd provided an alibi—a friend claimed they'd spent the evening together watching the Cubs game on TV, the same friend who had been with Bob during Doug's father's hunting accident. Doug had been away at a high school speech tournament, spending the weekend in a dorm room downstate. The story of his mother's death stayed in the news for several weeks, lingering longer than most, but eventually, like everything else in life, it faded.

Doug dials the number again. He isn't drunk anymore. In fact, he feels more lucid than he's ever felt. For the first time, he believes he can undo the terrible things that have happened, that he can turn time back, that he can control the outcome. On the eighth ring, a boy answers.

"Hello?" the boy whispers.

"Hello?" Doug says. "Hello? Who is this? Is this Dougie?" Doug knows without a doubt that he is speaking to his younger self. He doesn't even realize he's crying until his knuckles, wrapped around the receiver and pressed against his face, pool up the wetness.

"Who are you?" the boy asks. "Is this Mr. Belvedere?"

Doug takes a deep breath. The name is familiar. But why? "Who's Mr. Belvedere? Tell me about him."

"He's in a better place now," Dougie says.

"He's dead?" Doug asks. "Did someone kill him?"

"He's in a better place now," Dougie repeats.

"Listen," Doug says. "I don't have much time, and you won't hear from me again for another couple of years, so I want you to do something for me, okay? I want you to remember who I am. I want you to pay attention. Because something terrible is going to happen, and only you can stop it."

Dougie starts crying into the phone, and Doug remembers now how easily he used to fall apart, Uncle Bob always mocking him, matching little Dougie's snivels with his own fake snivels, mashing his ugly, scrunched-up face against Dougie's, his uncle's sour breath like poison. He could taste that man's breath for hours afterward.

"Don't cry, Dougie," Doug says. "Don't cry. I'm your friend. You have to believe me. I'm your friend. Okay? I'm your . . ." He senses something has happened. "Hello? Dougie? Hello?" The call has disconnected.

The phone calls are jumping in time, but by how much?

Doug quickly calls back, but the old phone is slow, and each number he dials on the rotary requires patience. It's one of the reasons he has continued using this old phone, to distinguish himself from his coworkers who are always distracted by their cell phones, texting even as he's trying to talk to them. "Go on," they'll say. "I'm listening." Doug thought the rotary phone would keep him grounded, but now he desires speed; he desires whatever technology will allow him to stay in contact with his old life.

"Hello?" It's the boy again. Dougie. Himself. His voice—the boy's—is deeper now.

"Dougie," Doug says. "How old are you?"

"Who is this?"

"Quick. How old are you?"

"Nine," Dougie says.

"Nine," Doug repeats. "Do you remember me? We talked probably three years ago? You had mentioned someone named Mr. Belvedere?"

"I don't know what you're talking about," Dougie says.

In the background, a man calls out, "Who the hell are you talking to? If they're selling something, just hang up!"

"Is that Uncle Bob?" Doug asks.

"Yes?" Dougie says. He's suspicious, but he's curious, too. Doug knows this because he knows how he would feel.

"Something terrible is going to happen to Mom," Doug says. He swallows. *Slow down*, he tells himself. "To your *mother*," Doug says. "I don't know who's responsible, but I think it's your Uncle Bob. It'll happen when you're fifteen."

His voice shaking, Dougie whispers, "I'm calling the police."

"It's too soon," Doug says. "He hasn't done anything yet."

"I'm calling them on *you*," Dougie says.

"No, no. I'm your friend."

"No, you're not," Dougie says and hangs up.

Doug dials the number again as fast as he can, as fast as the phone will allow him. It rings ten times. Eleven. Twelve. Thirteen. Has he wasted a phone call? What if time jumps six years the next time he calls? *Pick up . . . pick up*, he thinks. And then, miraculously, someone picks up. He can tell by the way the phone rattles, the way the receiver is almost dropped, that whoever picked up must have run to the phone.

"Yes? Hello?"

It's his mother. It's Shirley.

"Shirley?" Doug says.

"Yes?" She's out of breath.

Doug realizes that this may be the last time he'll ever talk to his mother. He also realizes that the phone he's using is the same phone his mother is using: the heavy black rotary. They are holding the same receiver, but they are separated by time and space.

He decides to risk it. He'll never forgive himself if he lets this moment go. "Mom," he says.

Shirley says, "I'm sorry, but . . ."

"No," Doug says. "It's me. It's Doug."

There is silence. Then Doug hears her digging through her purse to find her cigarettes. She keeps them in a rectangular pouch with a snap; there's a pocket on the side for the disposable butane lighter. He hears the flick of the lighter, his mother puffing to get the cigarette lit.

She exhales and says, "I knew it was you the first time you called all those years ago."

"How?" Doug asks. "How did you know?"

"A mother knows her son," she says.

Doug flips off his bedroom light and lies down, setting the phone on his chest.

Doug says, "I need to tell you something."

"Hold that thought?" his mother says, her voice getting higher as she ends her request as a question. "I want to know about you. I want to know how you've been. Did everything turn out okay?"

No, he thinks. *No, it hasn't*. But he doesn't want to disappoint her. "Everything's beautiful," Doug says.

"Are you married?"

"Yes," Doug lies.

"Kids?"

"A boy and a girl."

"Are they healthy?"

"Yes, they are," Doug says. "They're perfect."

"What's your wife's name?"

He imagines his coworker from earlier tonight, the way she would touch his ankle with her toes. "Louise," Doug says. "Louise Malgrave."

"I'm so happy," his mother says.

"But, Mom. Listen," Doug says.

His mother interrupts: "Shhhhhhhhh. Hush now. I want to hear about you."

Doug shuts his eyes. He's so tired. "I don't know what else there is to tell you."

"Tell me what your day is like. Tell me what you look like now," she says. "Tell me anything. I just want you to talk to me."

Doug obeys. He tells her of an imaginary day in the life of a Doug that doesn't exist. He tells her about his three-bedroom house. It's in a neighborhood she always wanted to live in. He tells her about the new riding lawn mower, the family portraits on the wall, the alligator shoes Louise bought him for his birthday. He tells her about the life she always dreamed of, the life he'll never live, and he can tell by the way she laughs or sighs that she's happy about how her son's future will turn out.

•

Doug wakes up with the phone on his chest, the receiver beeping near his ear. He'd fallen asleep while talking to his mother. His heart starts pounding. How could he have fallen asleep?

He reaches over and flips on the light. He hangs up the phone long enough to get a dial-tone and then dials his old number again. It barely rings before someone answers.

"Who is this?" It's Uncle Bob. His voice is deep, a rumble. He sounds as though he hasn't slept in days, weeks.

Doug says, "Can we talk?"

"I knew it," Uncle Bob says. "I just didn't think you'd have the gall to call here."

"You don't understand," Doug says.

In the background, Shirley says, "Who is it?" and Uncle Bob says, "You know damned well who it is."

"Hold on," Doug says. His own breathing is shallow. He feels sick. "I'm not who you think I am," he says. "Please listen to me."

Uncle Bob's voice comes to Doug from a distance now; he must have set down the receiver. "You want to talk to him one last time?" he asks Shirley. "Come here and talk to him," he yells.

"I don't know what you're talking about, Bob," Shirley says.

Something falls over and breaks. Shirley screams.

Doug, holding the phone, paces his bedroom. He's yelling into the receiver: "Bob! Bob! Bob, let's talk!"

Their voices, his mother's and Uncle Bob's, grow louder as they approach the phone, but it sounds as though his mother is being dragged against her will.

"Leave her alone!" Doug yells.

Clearly, Bob isn't listening. He's gripped by his own rage, the way a man drowning in quicksand can't think of anything except surviving. He says, "You want to talk to him? Hunh? You want to talk to him?"

The phone, Doug can tell, is being picked up. But then there is a loud crash coupled with a scream. The crash is like an explosion in Doug's ear. This sound repeats, over and over, until his mother stops screaming. He hears his uncle breathing heavily, and then he hears nothing, as though the phone's cord has been pulled from the wall. Doug waits.

But there's only silence. Just silence.

Doug hangs up and dials again. There's a noise after the second ring, a click, as though someone is answering, but it's only the familiar automated voice from years past: "We're sorry, but you've reached a number that's no longer in service . . ."

Doug slams the receiver back into place.

He sits on the edge of his bed, phone on his knee, shaking. He's cold, too. Freezing. He plays the last phone call over in his head and then plays it again, his uncle yelling, "You want to talk to him? Hunh? You want to talk to him?"

On a hunch, Doug lifts the phone into the air, holding the receiver to keep it secure in its place, and then flips the entire phone upside down. The bottom is black metal with perforations, four thick rubber washers for legs, stickers with numbers printed across them, a dial for turning the ringer up, and several screws. Doug feels it before he sees it. The tip of his finger hits a series of rough patches on the metal surface. Holding it close to the light, Doug can see it now: dried blood. He confirms it by chipping some away with his fingernail. It's been here all along, traveling with him from apartment to apartment, always next to him as he sleeps. Doug chips away more dried blood until his hands are covered with brown flecks and his fingertip is bleeding from scratching at the phone.

It's his mother's blood. It's his mother's blood, and Doug is holding the murder weapon.

Doug drops the phone onto his bed and walks to his kitchen, flipping on the light. He picks up the phone bill and studies it up and down, searching for an address. On the back of the last page is print so small, he isn't even sure in what language it's written. He pulls from his desk drawer a magnifying glass his mother had given to him when he was a child. It has a hand-carved ivory handle and sterling silver frame, and it had once belonged to her grandfather. Before handing it over, his mother had made Doug promise to be careful with it. Doug is depressed now to think he's kept it not on a mantel or wrapped in velvet but in a drawer littered with matchbooks, old IDs, orphaned keys, a furtive golf ball, and worthless wristwatches that died long ago.

He holds the magnifying glass up to his eye, moving it close to the text on the bill and then back up to his face, until the words come into focus. In the tiniest print, he sees a street address for customer complaints. The company is local, and their offices are located in a building downtown that he knows well: the Belvedere.

Doug leaves his apartment, the phone bill clutched in his fist. He's never been downtown this time of night, after the bars have closed. The stoplights are all blinking yellow for caution. There are, however, a surprising number of cars parked along the side streets. Doug takes the first space he sees, even though it's several blocks from the Belvedere.

Doug had lived with his Uncle Bob until he graduated high school and went away to college. During those two years after his mother's murder, Uncle Bob had taken surprisingly good care of Doug. In fact, he was kinder to Doug after his mother's death than he'd ever been when she was alive. It wasn't that violence ever had been visited upon Doug, nor did he ever see his uncle do anything to his mother. It was more of a mood that Doug was keenly aware of when his uncle was around, the way a rainy day might become eerily sunny and airless before a tornado. It was intangible. But all that stopped once his mother was gone. One evening, when Doug was nineteen and home for Christmas break, he walked upstairs to ask his uncle what he wanted for dinner. When he opened his uncle's bedroom door—his *mother's* bedroom door—he saw his uncle lying perfectly motionless on the bed, on his back, a white sheet pulled up to his neck, his skin already as gray as a midwestern sky in late November. Doug's first impulse was to call 9-1-1, but at the phone he paused. *It's too late*, he thought. *There's nothing to be done.* He sat on the side of the bed and spent time with the dead man before making the call.

It's cold out tonight, and Doug can't stop shivering. It's as though the convulsions are now part of his nervous system, utterly beyond his control, so he tightens his grip on the phone bill so as not to lose it when he trembles.

Doug rounds a corner, where the tall, slim Belvedere stands like a soldier among kneeling prisoners. He starts picking up his pace to reach the revolving door when he realizes that the building's plaza, with its manicured trees and freshly painted garbage cans, is crowded with dozens of people. He recognizes Mary Beemis, whose daughter disappeared one winter afternoon after school, never to be seen again. Across the way, he sees Mr. Simon, whose elderly father wandered away one night in the freezing cold—gone forever. In front of him stand the Garcia twins, now in their twenties, whose parents were killed in an unsolved hit-and-run. These are the city's grievers, its mourners, and they are all peering up at the Belvedere and whispering, as though praying to a temple of lost souls.

The phone bill slips from Doug's fingers, kisses the concrete, and then skitters down the paper-strewn street. He had thought he'd come here looking for answers, but he sees now that there are no answers. He is here for the same reason so many others are here—to let the past go, to move on. Out of breath, still trembling, Doug slowly crosses the street, where in the cold pre-dawn he joins ranks with his tribe of the bereaved, over a hundred others standing together, shoulder to shoulder, but utterly and forever alone.

THE CREEPING END
(a triptych)

1

The dead man was discovered in a parking garage stairwell, the same garage where Detective Jankowicz had found a lost pug thirteen years earlier during an ice storm. The dog had been shivering when the detective found it, its crooked teeth clacking, so he lifted the black pug off the concrete and zipped her up inside his jacket. Before he brought her home to show his wife, Sharon, he whispered to the dog, "You better be good, okay? If you're not good, she'll murder us both. I'm not shitting you, little dog."

The dead man in the parking garage was wearing a leather bomber jacket and Ray-Ban aviator sunglasses, but there was no wallet on his person. He had been shot once through the heart—that much was clear.

From the dead man's hand, Detective Jankowicz retrieved a cell phone to search for clues—it was the same model as his own cell phone—but the call history had already been erased, as had all the text messages. The detective swiped the screens back and forth, but there were no Google or Facebook apps on any of the screens. There was an address book full of hundreds of names and phone numbers, most of them accompanied by an avatar too small to see. Most significant were the photographs. There were thousands of them, and all of them were of a penis. From the angle that the photos had been taken, the penis presumably belonged to the owner of the cell phone. It was quite possibly, although not conclusively, the dead man's penis.

The detective scrolled and scrolled. Though the subject was the same, the photographer had made use of the camera phone's various features. The penis had a vintage look about it in some photos, while in others it was sepia or solarized. A few of the photos had been shot in negative, making the penis look otherworldly, like a photo Neil Armstrong might have taken of his own penis while sitting in a moon buggy. A few were wildly distorted, as though reflected in a funhouse mirror—bulbous at the top, pencil-thin at the base. There was an aqua penis, a cinnamon penis, a bleak penis. Most disturbing was the photo in which the man's penis was surrounded by an antique frame. It looked like a daguerreotype taken by a perverted prospector during the gold rush. An old-timey penis, Detective Jankowicz thought. In more photos than not, the penis was erect and firmly gripped in the man's hand, much as one would patriotically hold a flag while march-ing in a Fourth of July parade. It was, the detective had to admit, a large penis—or, at least, larger than his own—and he could almost understand why the man had taken so many. Each photo was like a hip business card that offered little more than an image that told you, in some oblique but evocative way, what the company had to offer, and if you wanted to know more, why, you simply asked the person who gave you the card.

The coroner said, "Well? Should we call it a day?" He was an old man with hands so gnarled and veiny, they looked like skin-covered tree bark. He and the detective were both atheists. The topic of God had come up one night in a bar after a few too many shots, but it wasn't some-thing they would ever mention in the light of day—not here in Winston-Salem, at least.

The detective pulled out his own cell phone and took several photos of the dead man. When he was done, he clapped the coroner on the back and said, "It's a day all right."

The detective, afraid that he would be blocked in by all the other emergency vehicles, had parked down a side street. It was bitterly cold out with a blank, grey-white sky overhead—much colder than one would think it could get in North Carolina. The sky was churning. Jankowicz thought, *It's going to snow*, and that's when he saw across the street a woman standing by herself.

The woman was in her thirties, thin, and had long black hair. She looked Southeast Asian. Possibly from Laos. Or Thailand. He'd had a Thai girlfriend in college. Nok. The woman across the street wasn't wearing a coat, so her arms were crossed, and she bounced lightly from foot to foot. She might have been waiting for someone, but it was difficult to determine intent. When she saw the detective looking at her, she cocked her head and then turned around, facing an abandoned storefront. The detective hesitated a moment before walking on.

Inside his unmarked squad car, he examined the phone again. There were over seven thousand photos of the man's penis—7,142, to be precise. The detective had taken an art class from a hippie in college who saw penises in every painting he showed them. "Look," he would say. "The phallus! Do you see it? The phallus is everywhere in this painting. Just look! It's here. And here. And here. And here. And here. And here. And over here." And for a while, the detective began to see penises everywhere he looked: the bottle he drank out of was a glass phallus, his own penis was an ironic phallus, the shoes he wore were two giant phalluses. *I'm wearing a couple of size twelve dicks*, he thought ruefully one morning as he tied their laces. He had begun pointing out penises to his girlfriend, Nok. "Look at the ice cream cone that little boy is holding," he said one night after they had left the movie theater. "It's a giant penis, and it's dripping!" He shivered. "Disgusting," he said, turning Nok away from the sight. Before spring break, Nok broke up with him. He could see it in her eyes when she started to speak. He knew it was coming. After she delivered the news, she reached over and pulled a thread off his shirt, as though cleaning him up before sending him out into the world alone.

The detective eventually quit attending the hippie's class, unable to see the value in recognizing phalluses everywhere he turned, and yet here he was now, almost thirty years later, a cell phone in his hand, and it was, as the professor had promised, a world full of phalluses. The hippie was onto something after all.

2

During the last six months that he and his wife lived together, before the separation, Detective Jankowicz developed a sensation inside his head that he could only describe as his brain shivering. His brain shivered, or so it seemed, inside its skull. What followed the shivering was a sensation of chemicals filling up his head, resulting in simultaneous feelings of euphoria and pending death. And then he'd wake up, trying to catch his breath.

The detective visited a neurologist, who thought he was having simple partial seizures and prescribed antiseizure medicine, but the medicine didn't stop the brain shivers from coming. They stopped only after he and his wife of twenty years separated. He wasn't even aware at first that they had stopped. He had been too preoccupied by the financial logistics of his divorce. He hadn't had a brain shiver, or whatever they had been, for a month by the time of his sleep study—a study he had scheduled for himself out of desperation—but he decided to keep his appointment anyway in case the shivers returned.

On the day that he was supposed to go—the evening of the day that he had worked the case of the dead man with the cell phone—the sleep study clinic shut down because of a freak snowstorm. In fact, the entire city of Winston-Salem had shut down, as though in the grips of a historical blizzard, though little more than an inch of snow had accumulated.

"We can reschedule you for next week," the receptionist told him over the phone. "Or, if you like, you can come in Saturday night. It'll be a reduced staff, though. And you may be the only patient here. But that's an option, honey."

Saturday night, Detective Jankowicz parked behind the clinic and, clutching his pillow, walked to the back door, which was lit by a single bulb. He was wearing his sleeping clothes—sweatpants and a T-shirt—

under his heavy coat. As soon as he rang the buzzer, the door opened. Had the man who opened the door been peering through the peephole the whole time, waiting for him to arrive?

"Hello, Detective. Let's get you in out of the cold." The man wore hospital scrubs and a stethoscope but was not a doctor. He reminded the detective of backwoods preachers he'd had dealings with: short and mustached with a high-pitched voice and a fierce light burning in his eyes. "I'll be taking care of you. Name's Thomas."

Thomas led the detective to a room that looked like a motel bedroom and motioned for him to sit in the room's sole chair. He explained that he would be hooking him up to all kinds of electrodes and wires and that he should relax. "Pretend you're getting a haircut," he added. He slipped over the detective's head a machine connected to a chain. The machine covered most of the detective's torso. Jankowicz felt ridiculous, as though he were a Halloween robot or an old school hip-hop artist wearing the most preposterously large medallion imaginable. How could he possibly sleep wearing a machine of this size?

"You're a homicide detective?" Thomas asked, and the detective nodded. "Well, now, that's something," Thomas said, plugging wires into the machine and then attaching the wires' electrodes to the detective's head. "And you've been involved in some big cases, too, now isn't that right?" he asked, rhetorically. "The Baldino murder in 2004? Now, that's a story, isn't it? Killed by a power drill? Oh, man." Thomas smiled and shook his head. "Or the case of Elaine Riggs. She smothered her twin boys in their sleep, right? How on *earth* does a mother do that to her own two children?" He sighed. "You're not from North Carolina originally, are you? From Chicago, right?"

Detective Jankowicz nodded. The only way that Thomas could have known any of this information, Jankowicz realized, was if he had googled the detective ahead of time. The detective was about to ask Thomas why he had googled him, if that was standard procedure before a visit to the sleep clinic, which the detective was pretty sure wasn't, when Thomas said, "Twice now, I've died and come back to life."

"I beg your pardon?"

"I saw you looking at the scars on my arms. You probably saw the scars on my head, too."

The detective had not noticed any scars at all until Thomas pointed them out, but now that they had been pointed out, it was impossible not to stare at them. The scars were thick, like putty attached to flesh.

"First time," Thomas said, "I fell off the roof of a house and was pronounced dead." He used to work as a handyman, he explained, and he used to drink on the job. His fatal descent began when he lost his footing on a steeply pitched roof. Thomas said, "I grabbed onto the lip of the gutter on my way off. Might as well've grabbed onto a razorblade." He held up his right hand. The tips of three fingers were missing. Why hadn't the detective noticed this before? Thomas leaned in close, his breath smelling of coffee and Certs. "Hit my head on the concrete and cracked open my skull. They pronounced me dead at the hospital. For three solid minutes, I was officially dead." He leaned back, put a hand on the detective's shoulder, and said, "Now, how many people can say that?" He averted his eyes, possibly out of embarrassment, and said, "Second time, I drank myself to death."

Jankowicz, who did not believe in an afterlife, was haunted by the nothingness that lay beyond him. Two years after his college girlfriend, Nok, had broken up with him, she died in a car accident, a head-on collision, with a drunk driver. Even now, he suspected her death had affected him more than he could ever admit, which was why he tried not to think about it.

"What was it like?" the detective asked. "Being dead?"

Thomas remained silent while he attached the final electrodes, and then he said, "Does Detective Jankowicz need to pee before he goes beddy-bye?"

The detective nodded, and Thomas helped him off the chair and led him down a corridor to a restroom. Inside, Jankowicz caught sight of himself in the mirror. He looked like something from a science fiction movie—part man, part machine, his innards a tangle of wires, his chest a circuit board. How the hell was he supposed to piss, he wondered as he fumbled with the sweatpants' elastic band, unable to see beyond the wires. He finally gave up and shuffled back to the fake bedroom.

"Okay, now," Thomas said, helping the detective to the bed. "If you want to stay up for a while, you can do that. Here's the light switch. Make yourself comfortable. I'll be in another room monitoring you. There's a P.A., so if I need something, I'll speak to you through the P.A. If *you* need something, just ask me. I'll be here all night. In point of fact, we're the only two living souls here."

Jankowicz tried to get comfortable on the bed but couldn't with all the rigging around his head. He noticed a video camera mounted to a wall and wondered if Thomas would be staring at him for six straight hours, occasionally jotting down notes.

On his way out, Thomas paused for a long, almost loving look toward the detective. "It's how I'd always imagined it," he finally said. "Only better."

"What?" the detective asked.

"Death," Thomas said. He said, "I can hardly wait for the third time." He peered up at the room's ceiling vent, as though tucked away inside the vent's darkness were the secrets of the universe, and said, "Praise Jesus."

Unable to move comfortably and certain he would not sleep for even a minute, Jankowicz said, "Amen."

3

Among the over seven thousand photos on the dead man's phone was one that was not of the man's penis. It was of a woman sitting on a park bench and smiling at the photographer. She looked foreign, possibly Thai, and she was wearing sunglasses on top of her head. He had seen her before, this woman. She had been standing across the street from the parking garage. Why hadn't the detective gone over to speak to her when he'd had the chance? Was the divorce making him unable to read people the way he had once been able to? In the photo, the woman's eyes betrayed the smile, and Detective Jankowicz loaded the photo onto his computer at work so that he could enlarge the image.

The woman sat on the bench with her knees almost touching but not quite, her hands clasped in her lap. It wasn't fear in her eyes, but it wasn't happiness, either. They were eyes the detective had seen before, back in college, when his girlfriend Nok told him it wasn't going to work out between them. Her eyes, he remembered, told the whole story, expressing genuine sadness but also relief. *It's over*, the eyes said. *It's finally over*.

The detective's screen saver had come on, and he was rubbing the bridge of his nose when the phone on his desk rang. It was his wife—his soon to be ex-wife—Sharon.

"Yeah?" he said, trying to make his voice as emotionless as possible. This was new to him, talking to her as though she were just anyone at all.

"It's Alice," Sharon said. "She's not doing well."

Alice was their stocky black pug that had been riddled with health problems for years—mast cell tumors, arrhythmia, two back legs that no longer worked. Her latest health issue involved her jaw. The bones in a pug's jaw were frail to begin with, but after years of grinding down food with crooked teeth in a too-small mouth, the jaw bones had become as thin as floss. Their vet, Dr. Lannigan, had repaired the first fracture months ago, but he had warned them that it might not hold.

"I'll be right over," Jankowicz said.

When Sharon opened the front door of the small house she had rented after the separation, she was holding a pillow with the old dog resting upon it, the way a child princess would be carried around the royal court. For the first time ever, the dog did not acknowledge Jankowicz's presence. Her eyes, unfocused but moving quickly, laid bare the pain.

Jankowicz reached out to scratch the old dog's head, careful not to bump the dog's lower jaw. The jaw hung all the way open while the dog's tongue, a slab of dry flesh, futilely attempted to aid the throat in swallowing. Sharon wasn't crying, but the skin under her eyes was puffy and wrinkled, and her nose was chapped from having repeatedly wiped it.

"I think it's time," Jankowicz said, and Sharon nodded. "Why don't you bring her to the house in a few hours. I'll call the vet's office, make sure they can get her in right away."

What Jankowicz didn't say, but what they both knew, was that he needed to go home first to dig a hole. He was always stunned how difficult it was to dig deeper than a few shovelfuls of dirt. He'd have to dig deep enough so that the body wouldn't be excavated by whatever wild animal scurried near the grave, catching a whiff of death. He had buried four dogs in his lifetime. Alice would be the fifth. Fortunately, the temperature had risen considerably the last few days, and the melted snow softened the ground.

Detective Jankowicz was standing in the driveway when Sharon arrived.

"Want me to drive?" he asked, and she nodded.

They took his unmarked patrol car to the vet's office. Alice lay on a towel on his wife's lap. The detective drove without speaking, but every now and again he would reach over and scratch the top of the pug's head. Whatever had gone wrong in his marriage had gone wrong years ago, so there was no point in analyzing or discussing it. They'd both agreed that relationships had an expiration point, and they'd lived long enough to reach theirs: twenty years.

It took ten minutes to reach the vet's office. The harder Jankowicz tried concentrating on what was going to happen to Alice, the more vividly he saw instead the Thai woman on the bench. He thought of her eyes, sad and relieved. He wondered who she was or if he could ever find her. He wondered if she would know who killed the man who had taken her photo. He wondered, not unreasonably, if she had killed him.

The detective helped Sharon out of the car by lifting from her lap the towel with Alice wrapped inside, but Sharon wanted to continue holding the dog so he handed the bundle back to her and opened the door of the lobby. The one thing Jankowicz never got used to in his job was the smell of death, and the dog's putrid breath hinted at the creeping end.

The receptionists already knew Alice's fate when they walked in, and the three of them, wearing stiff blouses with cartoon dogs and cats on them, stood together behind the counter to greet Alice.

"Such a good girl," they said to her, reaching over to touch her one last time.

"We're so sorry," one of them said to the detective and his wife. "How old is Miss Alice?"

"Fourteen, fifteen years," the detective said. "We're not really sure."

"He found her in a parking garage," his wife added, motioning toward her husband. "He saved her life."

The door to the hallway that led to the exam rooms opened, and a young vet tech asked them to follow her. The detective was aware of the dog's time ticking down, that this would be the last time she would travel this hallway, the last time she would enter this exam room and lie upon this steel table, the last time she would be with the people she considered, in whatever mysterious way she considered things, to be hers.

Normally they would have had to wait, but Dr. Lannigan stepped inside right away. He was a bald, tan man in his late fifties, and he stopped as soon as he saw the dog that he had brought back from the precipice so many times, this dog he called his miracle pug. Today, however, he said very gently, "You've had enough of this world, haven't you?" He walked over to Alice and put his bald head against her graying head and whispered, "It's okay. You've been a good girl."

The detective looked up at Sharon, whose eyes were wet now. She pulled a Kleenex from her purse and blew her nose. The detective was holding it together, not giving in to what he felt, but then Dr. Lannigan wiped his eyes, and the detective thought, *oh, shit*, but still he managed not to cave. All three of them put their hands on the animal as though she were a sacred thing in possession of restorative powers. Then the vet pulled from his pocket two syringes—one to make the dog slip into sleep, the other to make the dog slip into death.

While Dr. Lannigan tried to find a vein in the dog's bony arm, the detective held the dog around her torso, his thumb pressing in the exact spot of the dog's heart. The heart was thumping harder than usual. When a door slammed in another part of the building, the pug jerked up to see what was happening. *She's aware*, the detective thought. *She knows what we're doing to her*. He tightened his grip on her and said, "Shhh, it's okay, sweetie, it's okay."

The side of his hand touched the side of his wife's hand, the first time their skin had touched in months. The dog's heart sped up as the doctor punctured her skin and injected the first liquid.

"She's going to go to sleep now," he said, and he ran his hand across her head, as a magician might, as the dog lost consciousness.

The doctor said, "Okay," and he inserted the second syringe into her leg. He barely pushed the plunger with his thumb, filling her vein, when the old dog's heart stopped beating. The detective waited for another beat, but it never came. "It's done now," the doctor said. "She's gone."

Sharon wrapped the towel around the dead dog, and then the detective lifted the swathed pug and carried it out to the lobby while his wife stayed behind to take care of the bill. This was, Jankowicz understood, the last thing he and Sharon would ever do together as husband and wife. His hands, he saw now as he reached to pull open the door, were caked with dirt and clay from the enormous hole he had dug. He had dug deep and wide enough to bury not just the dog but to bury all three of them. He had dug in proportion to his grief.

He popped the trunk and gently set the dog inside atop paperwork for murders he was still working, mysteries that no one had yet solved. Cold cases. After he shut the trunk and leaned against the car to wait for his wife, he answered the buzzing phone in his pocket.

"Hello?" he said.

"*Sawasdee kha*," a woman said, and Jankowicz felt dizzy.

Although he had not seen her in almost thirty years, he knew the sound of her voice as well as he knew his own. It was his college girlfriend, Nok. But how was that possible? She had died when she was twenty-four. The detective had gone to the funeral in Murphysboro. He had helped carry the coffin to the hearse, and he had watched as it was lowered into the ground.

"You don't love me," Nok said now. "Why you don't call? I worry."

"Yes," he said, his eyes blurring at last. "Of course I still love you. Where are you?" He swallowed. Was this really happening? Shyly, he asked, "Can I see you again?"

There was silence. Then the line went dead. When he looked down at the phone's screen, the detective saw that he was holding the dead man's phone and not, as he had thought, his own, and when he pulled up the information about who had called, he saw the photo of the Thai woman sitting on the park bench, her eyes staring back at him. He had made so many mistakes lately. What he had mistaken for sadness and relief in her eyes were only reflections of the day's clouds.

The detective, wiping clean his face, composed himself. He hadn't eaten much today or had any water to drink. He would call this woman back later tonight and break the news. He would ask her to meet him for coffee so that he might ask her some questions. He would take his own photo of her with his phone, but he won't be sure of his motives for doing so. One day, perhaps not as far in the future as Jankowicz would wish, a stranger would find, among the many photos of dead people still populating the detective's phone, a single image of this Thai woman. *Who is she?* the stranger might wonder. Who is she, and what could this beautiful woman possibly have meant to a sad and rumpled man whose final breath had already dispersed in the air around them?

THE BLUEPRINT OF YOUR BRAIN

One month ago, Jimmy Presko accidentally burned down his parents' new garage. He was twelve years old. A pile of charred debris now sat in their driveway, and you could smell what had burned and melted from several blocks away. His mother sat across from him, snipping an article from the newspaper with her toenail scissors. All the articles she saved looked like doilies because of the curved blades of the scissors. Every few minutes, Jimmy's father appeared out the living room's bay window, pushing the lawnmower and smoking. He hadn't spoken much to Jimmy since the fire episode. Jimmy didn't blame him, really.

"Look at this," Jimmy's mother said, handing over one of her scalloped-edge newspaper clippings. The story was about a new program for latchkey kids. If a girl or boy came home from school and started feeling lonely or frightened or sad, all she or he had to do was pick up the phone, dial zero, and say to the operator, "Grandma, please!" to speak to an elderly woman or "Grandpa, please!" to speak to an elderly man. A moment later, the child would be connected. According to the mayor, who spearheaded the program, it served two goals: it provided a sense of comfort for the rudderless kids in town, and it gave meaning to the lives of forgotten retirees, who were lonely themselves and felt that their connection to society was slipping through their fingers. "It's a win-win," the mayor was quoted as saying.

His mother said, "Pin that to the fridge, okay?" When Jimmy said nothing, his mother said, "Remember, just pick up the phone, dial zero, and say, 'Grandpa, please!'"

Jimmy stared outside, where his father ran over a tennis ball that Jimmy had forgotten to pick up. The ball shot out of the lawnmower's side as though from a batting cage pitching machine. When the shredded ball whacked the bay window, Jimmy's mother jumped, but Jimmy didn't so much as flinch.

"Okay," Jimmy said to his mother. "'Grandpa, please.' Got it."

•

The following Saturday, for the first time since the fire, Jimmy's parents left him alone while they went shopping at Home Depot. At first Jimmy spent time staring at his hands until they began to freak him out. It was grotesque the way each hand had sprouted fingers, and if that wasn't enough, each finger was a different length. On closer inspection, he noticed fine blonde hair up and down each finger, hair that was barely noticeable right now, but he imagined it growing thicker as he aged, until both hands looked like his mother's white cashmere gloves. The thought made him queasy and sad in equal measures.

Jimmy reached into his pocket and pulled out the new smartphone his parents had bought him. He pressed zero. When the operator, an elderly woman, answered, Jimmy said, "Grandpa, please."

"Oh," the operator said. "Oh, yes. Hold on, honey."

Jimmy waited patiently through a series of clicking sounds, breathing in through his nose the awful smell of the burnt garage. An old man finally came on the line and said, "Yeah? Who is this?"

"Jimmy Presko," Jimmy said.

"Jimmy Presko, Jimmy Presko." There was silence. Then, "Do I know you? Are you trying to sell me something? Because if you are, you can go to hell, Jimmy Presko."

"No, sir." Jimmy wanted to explain about the news article, but the entire story, his reason for calling, suddenly seemed pathetic now, so all he replied was, "Grandpa, please?"

"Grandpa?" the old man said. "What the . . . oh, wait. You're one of those whatchamacallits."

"Latchkey kids."

The old man laughed. "That's right. *Latchkey.* Jesus, they've got a name for everything nowadays, don't they? *Latchkey*, for God's sake. Are you *sad?*" he asked. "Is that it? Are you *lonely?*" He laughed. "Well, boo hoo."

Jimmy said, "I burned down my parents' garage."

"Well, now I'm impressed," the old man said. "A firebug, eh?" He cleared his throat. "Listen. I need a favor. You think you can do something for me?"

As the old man explained what he wanted, Jimmy's mood lifted. He felt as though he were being pulled up out of a giant vat of molasses and hosed clean. It was, he hoped, a new beginning.

•

A day before the fire, Jimmy had been looking through a stack of 78 rpm records that were stored inside the cabinet of his father's old Brunswick upright phonograph. The phonograph, which had belonged to Jimmy's great-grandfather, was almost a hundred years old, and Jimmy loved putting an Andrew Sisters record on the turntable or one by Doris Day or another by Les Paul, and he loved turning the phonograph's crank exactly eighteen times and then pulling the lever that allowed the turntable to spin. He even loved replacing the needle after every two plays.

That Sunday, Jimmy found a record by Buddy Rich titled *Oop-Bop-Sha-Bam*. Jimmy didn't know that Buddy Rich was a drummer until he googled him after listening to the song and then watched on YouTube some of the craziest drumming he'd ever seen. He watched a dozen Buddy Rich videos and then sat outside in a lawn chair, pretending to be Buddy Rich by wildly flailing his arms and pumping an invisible pedal.

His father stepped outside, took a long look at Jimmy, and said, "Don't do that. It looks ridiculous," and then continued on to the garage.

Within seconds, Jimmy could see puffs of smoke escaping from an open window: his father sneaking a smoke.

The next day at school, Jimmy could barely pay attention. He kept hearing his father's words: *Don't do that. It looks ridiculous.* Each time he heard the words, his stomach tightened, and he felt like crying. When he got home, he rolled the old Brunswick upright phonograph into the garage and dropped a lit match into it. The match did nothing but burn itself out, so he set a roll of paper towels on fire, intending to put the roll inside the phonograph. But the paper towels lit up too fast, and he dropped them onto a pile of rags his father had used to varnish a table. The flames rose to the ceiling almost instantly.

Jimmy had learned in school that a house fire doubled in size every minute, but he hadn't grasped the magnitude of that fact until he watched the fire spread. It was hypnotic to watch, like a swirling carnival ride that keeps swooping closer and closer to your head. Finally, he ran to the house, dialed 9-1-1, and then stood outside and watched the flames.

By the time the fire engines arrived, the garage had caved in.

•

The old man's name was Perry, and what he wanted was a carton of Lucky Strikes. The carton was to be tied to a long string and tossed over a high stone wall at an address Perry had provided. If Jimmy felt two tugs on the string, he was to cut the line. Any deviation—or no tugs at all—and Jimmy was to abort the mission, pull the carton back over the wall and try again the next day at the same time.

Jimmy knew it would be impossible to find a carton of Lucky Strikes, but his father smoked Virginia Slims, and he smoked more than he admitted to Jimmy's mother. He used to store them in the garage, but now that the garage was gone, his father had to be more creative, storing them inside old Folgers coffee cans in the plastic storage shed in the backyard or in the basement, behind the furnace. Jimmy gathered up all the packs he could find and put them in a shoebox. To make up for them being the wrong kind, Jimmy added a blueberry muffin left over from breakfast and a paperback copy of *Everything You Always Wanted to Know about Sex*, which his parents kept hidden on the bookshelf behind a stack of old *National Geographic* magazines. He used duct tape to secure the shoebox's lid and then tied fishing line around the box. The fishing line was still attached to the fishing pole so that he could cast the box of goods over the wall.

And this was what he did, at precisely the time he had been told to do it. He hoped no one walking by noticed him standing there, a boy holding a fiberglass fishing pole with a line that went up and over a stone wall. He waited and waited. His upper lip grew a mustache of sweat. Just as he considered reeling the box back toward him, he felt two tugs. Jimmy pulled his mother's toenail scissors from his pants pocket and snipped the fishing line.

Later that day, while his father was busy eyeing his mother with great suspicion, Jimmy called the phone number that Perry had given him.

"Yeah?" Perry said.

"It's me," Jimmy said. "It's Jimmy."

"Jimmy the fisherman," Perry said. "I like the way you think."

Jimmy smiled. Had anyone ever told him they liked the way he thought? He didn't think so.

"But Virginia Slims?" Perry asked. "What kind of man smokes Virginia Slims? And a sex manual?" Perry sighed. "I don't know, Jimmy, I don't know. A Mickey Spillane novel would have been nice." Jimmy felt a burning behind his eyes, the unexpected heat of approaching tears. But Perry laughed and said, "Still and all, you done good, kid. *Damn* good."

"Thank you, sir," Jimmy said.

"Now, listen," said Perry. "There's something else I want you to do for me. Whaddaya say, Jimmy? You in?"

"Yes, sir. I'm in."

"That's my boy," Perry said. "That's my Jimmy."

•

The "something else" Perry wanted Jimmy to do turned out to be not one but many things, yet Perry clearly saw it as a single favor chopped up over several weeks. What he wanted was for Jimmy to go wherever Perry told him to go and then call and listen to him talk. At the end of it all, Perry promised, there would be a great big surprise.

Four days after the cigarette drop, Jimmy was to go to a small house in an older, rundown part of town. Jimmy rode his bike there after school, using the GPS on his smartphone to find it. After parking across the street, he sat on the curb and waited for Perry to call.

"You there?" Perry asked before Jimmy could say hello.

"Uh-huh."

Jimmy heard Perry lighting a cigarette.

"Virginia Slims or not," Perry said, "this cigarette is damned good. Haven't smoked in thirty years, son." He blew into the mouthpiece. The sound entered Jimmy as though the old man were blowing smoke directly into his ear, and Jimmy shivered. After a brief coughing fit, Perry told him the story of the tiny house, how he had been born in the rented basement in 1932 and slept in an open dresser drawer with blankets. His first memory was of riding a very large dog around the basement when he was one or two.

"I loved that dog. A white shepherd with a tongue the size of my head. A longhaired dog as white as snow. Eighty-five pounds. Beautiful animal, Jimmy. My first word was *bark*, for chrissakes," he said.

Perry smoked another cigarette and then another, telling stories about his parents—his long-suffering mother ("a damned saint, that woman") and his father, who was a Bible salesman one year and a patent medicine salesman the next. Once the Depression came, his father had to sell pretty much everything they owned.

"He let the dog loose," Perry said. "Couldn't afford to feed it. I was bawling my eyes out when my father pulled me toward him and said, 'Look, I had to make a choice. Feed the dog or feed you. I chose you, so quit your crying. I could have chosen the dog.'"

Jimmy listened to the rest of Perry's story, but what he saw in his own head was a chubby-armed baby astride a galloping white shepherd, and then he pictured the dog taking flight, like the winged white stallion Pegasus, while the baby's face lit up with joy. His shoulders shuddered at the thought of seeing something so beautiful, and he feared an unexpected desire to cry would overtake him. But then Perry started humming. It was a song Jimmy recognized, but he couldn't place it.

"Okay, kiddo," Perry said. "Tomorrow then. You know where to go."

Clearing his throat so his voice wouldn't crack, Jimmy said, "I do."

He expected Perry to ask him how he was doing, but the phone went dead, leaving Jimmy alone in a strange neighborhood as the sun dropped mercilessly from view.

•

"I want a white shepherd," Jimmy told his parents that night. His mother, sitting on the recliner with her legs propped up, toenail scissors in hand, looked up from her pile of clipped coupons.

His father, who stood at the dry bar capping a bottle of whiskey, glared at his son as though Jimmy were a stranger who had walked into his house uninvited. Then he motioned with a couple of fingers for Jimmy to come closer.

"Have you taken up smoking?" he asked Jimmy, leaning in so Jimmy's mother couldn't hear the question. It was almost the first thing his father had said to him that wasn't about him setting the garage on fire.

THE FEAR OF EVERYTHING

"No. Why?" Jimmy whispered.

The two continued making eye contact until his father sighed and said loudly, "What's this white shepherd business? What the hell even *is* a white shepherd?"

"It's a dog. And it would keep me company," Jimmy said. He paused for dramatic effect. "When you're not home," he added.

The look Jimmy's mother gave Jimmy's father suggested that telepathic communication was happening. She had already bought Jimmy an Xbox after he'd burned down the garage as an apology for leaving him alone for so long after school. Apparently, she had hoped the Xbox would keep him occupied until she and his father returned from work, but the reason he'd burned down the garage wasn't because he was lonely. He had been angry. And he was still angry. How could an Xbox fix that? But then Jimmy's father said, "Goddamn it, Mary. Okay, okay. I'll go to the pound tomorrow and see what they have." When his mother wasn't looking, Jimmy's father whispered, "But if I find out you're smoking, the dog is a goner. You got it?"

Jimmy nodded. "A goner," he said. "Got it."

•

Perry's next adventures for Jimmy included trips to Perry's old grammar school, his high school, and the house of his first girlfriend, Marguerite Drake. The grammar school was now a subdivision of houses called Botany Woods; the high school was a Kroger grocery store; but the house was still a house. Jimmy sat on a curb across from the house where young Marguerite Drake had lived.

"I've been reading that book you gave me," Perry said. "The sex manual. I could have used it back then, let me tell you. Did you know that the Chinese used powdered rhinoceros horns as an aphrodisiac?"

"No, sir," Jimmy said. "I didn't know that."

"Me neither," Perry said.

While Perry described the house as he remembered it—its green cedar shakes, the ivy creeping up a side wall—Jimmy studied the rotted wood and overgrown weeds. The roof, covered in patches of moss, looked as though it had a skin disease, and a cracked window had been taped back together.

"Marguerite was a beauty," Perry said. "Looked like Colleen Moore. Not that you know who the hell Colleen Moore is. Silent film actress. Big eyes, dark eyebrows. One of the first flappers—you know, with that bobbed pageboy haircut. You don't have any idea what I'm talking about, do you?" He blew smoke into the mouthpiece and said, "You got a girl, Jimmy?"

"Nope."

"What're you waiting for?" Perry yelled. "Hell, you should have one steady girl and half a dozen on the side."

"Okay," Jimmy said.

"Well, okay then," Perry confirmed. "It's done."

The curtains covering the front room moved, and someone peeked out. Could it have been Marguerite, now in her eighties but still waiting for Perry to return to her? Jimmy waved, but the curtain fell back into place, and Perry hung up without saying another word.

•

At school, Jimmy worked on overcoming his shyness by flirting with those girls other boys shunned. Their suffocating enthusiasm at Jimmy's advances, however, made them seem desperate, even mentally unbalanced, so Jimmy eventually turned his attention to the most popular girl in seventh grade: Lisa Muldoon.

Lisa Muldoon had brown hair and brown eyes, and her hair was long enough to be cut to look like the silent movie star Colleen Moore's, which he'd seen when he'd googled photos of the actress. Lisa was having a birthday that week, and, as was customary, there would be a party for her during lunch hour.

But that was two days away, and Perry had more "first" places for Jimmy to visit—the now-decrepit Miller's Hardware, home to Perry's first job and still open for business; a forest preserve (now a housing development) where Perry had first kissed Marguerite; Perry's first apartment after leaving home, located above Linwood Pharmacy.

As Perry smoked and talked, Jimmy imagined what these places must have looked like sixty years ago. In his mind, the images were always black and white, like photographs he'd seen of his grandparents, and the songs that played in the background were the records that had been stored inside the upright Brunswick's cabinet—"I Don't Hurt Anymore" by Dinah Washington or "The Tap Room Polka" by Six Fat Dutchmen— records he was starting to regret having burned up.

Perry said, "Next came Korea. But we'll talk about that tomorrow. I'm tired, Jimmy. It's not good, kid, being this tired all the time."

Jimmy wanted to say something about being tired, too, but Perry had already hung up.

•

The next day, Jimmy's father came home with a dog. The dog was white, but that's where the similarities between it and Perry's shepherd ended. While Perry's shepherd must have been eighty pounds, this one looked about ten. Eleven pounds tops.

Jimmy was sitting on the couch, eating pretzels from a bag. He stopped eating and said, "What's that?"

"It's your dog," his father said, still holding the leash.

Jimmy said, "It's not a white shepherd."

"You know what?" Jimmy's father said. "Sometimes people go to the car dealership wanting to buy a red two-door car, but all they've got in stock is a blue four-door. So that's what people buy. That's how the world works, Jimmy."

"What kind of dog is it?" Jimmy asked.

"A miniature American Eskimo."

"Isn't that a person?" Jimmy asked.

His father said, "Does it look like a person?" He shook his head, let go of the leash, and walked out of the room.

The dog walked over to Jimmy and sat down. It was as though someone had put Perry's dog in a machine and shrunk it. Jimmy handed it a pretzel and watched the dog eat. And then he handed him another. And another.

"Come up here, Perry," he said, naming the dog after the old man. He patted the couch, and the dog jumped up next to Jimmy and sat down—and there they remained for the next hour or so, eating pretzels together like two old friends.

•

Construction on the new garage had begun. Perry the dog watched out the front window and barked incessantly as workers tromped across the driveway and yard. Jimmy's father, whenever he came into the room, would give appraising looks at Jimmy and the miniature American Eskimo, as though they were a pair of impulsively purchased end tables that he couldn't make up his mind about. His mother, on the other hand, had begun to treat Jimmy gently, often asking if there was anything he needed. Jimmy wondered if his mother knew something about Jimmy's life expectancy that she couldn't bring herself to tell him. Only the dog really understood Jimmy, dutifully lumbering along beside him, waiting for his next pretzel.

Jimmy worried Perry the old man would ask him to travel overseas next. Jimmy couldn't do that, of course. He was already pushing his limits as it was, biking into neighborhoods that his parents had forbidden him to go into. A trip to Korea would be out of the question.

•

On the day of Lisa Muldoon's birthday, Jimmy wrapped his unopened Xbox in silver wrapping paper he'd found in his mother's closet. It was Christmas paper, but there were no words on it, no smiling Santas, only his own warped reflection and Perry the dog's as he affixed a red bow to the present.

"What do you think, Perry?" Jimmy asked, showing him the wrapped package.

The dog panted, shut his mouth, then panted some more.

At school, near the end of the celebration, after everyone had given Lisa gifts of lip gloss or heart-shaped candy, Jimmy retrieved the giant box—which he'd managed to get to school by balancing on his handlebars and which he'd hidden inside the supply closet—and set it down in front of her. Her eyes widened at the size of the box. He expected her to open it demurely, maybe even bashfully, but once she found a seam with one of her long nails, she clawed the paper away in two violent motions. When she saw what it was, she threw her arms around Jimmy's neck. Jimmy whispered into her ear, "Will you be my girlfriend?"

Instead of answering, Lisa kissed Jimmy on the cheek in front of all their classmates, including boys who had been unsuccessfully wooing Lisa since preschool, boys who could easily have pummeled Jimmy if they had wanted to, but right now everyone was too transfixed by the extravagance of Jimmy's gift and by Lisa's uncharacteristic enthusiasm. She looked down at the Xbox again, clenched her fists, and squealed so loud that everyone took a step back, as though a monster were in their midst.

•

After her birthday, Lisa shadowed Jimmy everywhere, as he had hoped she would, but mostly she talked about the Xbox—how great it was, how it was the best present ever, better than anything her parents had ever bought her. When Jimmy told her that he had another present for her, she punched his arm.

"Get real!" she said. And then she hugged him.

"Kind of a present that's also a favor," he said. "For me."

Once they were inside the hair salon and Lisa saw that the next present was a haircut, she was less than thrilled. And not just any haircut but a flapper's haircut. Bangs cut straight across the forehead, long commas of hair across the ears, all of it flattened down like ink. Jimmy showed her a photo of Colleen Moore and said, "Her father built her a dollhouse that was twelve feet high." Lisa smiled at this information and then slid into the beautician's chair.

Jimmy, imagining what Perry might say and do, said, "I'll be outside, kitten. Ring me if you need me." He held a hand up to his ear, thumb and forefinger extended, and then jiggled his hand. He winked at the beautician and then walked outside and leaned against a wall, the way he imagined guys used to do.

•

As it turned out, Perry didn't ask Jimmy to go to Korea. Where Perry asked him to go instead was the Greyhound bus station, where Perry had departed to Fort Riley in Kansas before shipping off to Korea.

When Jimmy showed up at Lisa's house wearing his mother's oversized sunglasses and walking Perry with a harness, Lisa said, "Why are you wearing women's sunglasses?"

Jimmy explained that he was spending as much time with his dog Perry outside school as possible and that he figured he probably couldn't bring a dog into the bus station unless it was a service dog, so that was why he was wearing dark glasses and why he needed Lisa to lead him into the station by the elbow.

"You're so weird," Lisa said. "But cute."

At the station, Jimmy was startled that no one else was there, not even an attendant selling tickets. The only light in the room came from the sun peeping through the big, dusty windows.

Jimmy pulled out his phone and called Perry.

"You there?" Perry asked. "At the station?"

"Yes, sir."

Perry said, "I was so glad to get the hell away from my old man, I didn't care if I was going to get shot at. Have I told you how the son of a bitch used to beat me?"

Jimmy didn't say anything. He kept the dark sunglasses on and listened. Lisa Muldoon strolled over to an old cigarette machine and pulled on its knobs, and then she danced for a while like a flapper, as Jimmy had taught her to do the night before while he hummed "Crazy Rhythm."

Jimmy kept waiting for Perry to take him through basic training at Fort Riley and then combat in Korea, but Perry's sole subject was his father.

"One time," Perry said, "I couldn't walk for a week. You know why? He would pick me up and throw me across the room. I was that small. Pick me up like a pillow and toss me." There was a pause, then Perry said, "Ah, Christ, I need another cigarette."

Lisa Muldoon slid from the wall to the floor and, widening her eyes, gave Jimmy a look of bored desperation. She poked out her bottom lip and traced her fingers along the commas of hair on either side of her head.

But Jimmy couldn't abandon Perry, so he switched the old man to speakerphone, then walked over to where Lisa was sitting. She patted the space next to her, and Jimmy sat. He knew it wasn't going to be easy to keep a girl like Lisa happy, this girl who was used to being surrounded by dozens of boys who wanted to keep her happy, but today at least, while

Perry the dog slept curled by a bench and Perry the old man's voice filled the empty room, Jimmy kissed every inch of Lisa's face and neck, saving her glossy, root beer-tasting lips for last.

•

Jimmy made a list of things Perry had mentioned in passing—things Perry had once owned, things he used to wear—and at the top of that list was a brown fedora. And so on a gray Saturday morning, Jimmy took Perry the dog to the Goodwill, tied Perry's leash to a bike rack, and entered the store with an image of a brown fedora already glowing on his cell phone. He flashed his phone to a man who worked at the store, the way he'd seen FBI agents on TV flash their badges, and the employee solemnly led him to a rack full of hats. Hanging from its wire branches like Christmas ornaments were ugly mesh ball caps and fluorescent caps made of fake satin, but planted on top of the rack, like an angel on a tree, was a brown fedora.

Although Perry had never mentioned shoes, Jimmy decided to buy a pair. Surely Perry wouldn't have worn gym shoes with his fedora. He'd remembered his father calling Florsheim top-of-the-line, so that's what Jimmy wanted, and after picking through several dozen pairs of crusty shoes, Jimmy finally found a pair. They were blue, and Jimmy loved them.

Jimmy wore the fedora and blue Florsheim shoes everywhere. The shoes were at least a few sizes too big, so he wore a pair of winter socks over his regular socks, even though the heat caused his feet to sweat and itch.

His mother said, "Honey, where did you get those?" and Jimmy shrugged.

"Don't worry," he said. "I bought 'em with my own jack."

"Jack?"

Jimmy sighed. "Money."

"You bought your own shoes?"

"Yeah. It was duck soup." His mother stared blankly at him, so he added, "Easy peasy lemon squeezy."

His teachers began calling him Mr. Presko. Out of respect, Jimmy figured. If you carried yourself with dignity, you got treated accordingly. This was something Perry had told Jimmy early on. Meanwhile, all Lisa Muldoon wanted to do was kiss. It didn't matter where they were—playground, homeroom, gymnasium.

"Kiss me, Jimmy," she said when he was on his way to the water fountain one day. "Please?"

"Not right now, doll. Later."

As for Perry, he skipped Korea altogether. When Jimmy broached the subject, Perry cut him short. "Korea's over," he said. "1965, Jimmy. That's where we are now. Got it?"

Jimmy sat with Perry the dog across the street from East River Savings and Loan—an old stone building with a corner entrance. Above the entrance was an ancient brass clock that still worked. Chiseled into stone above the door was a Roman numeral: MDCCCXCII. Jimmy tried figuring out the year but gave up at the letter "D."

Perry said, "Imagine, if you will, hunger. A string of lousy jobs after the war. Disillusionment. Nothing—and I mean *nothing*—going your way. They said I was shell-shocked, that that's why I couldn't keep a job, but I wasn't buying it. Didn't then and still don't. I got bored easily, Jimmy. You ever get bored?"

"Yes, sir."

"You ever been depressed?"

"I don't know."

Perry started humming that song again, the one he'd hummed before. The words almost came to Jimmy, but then they didn't. It was like having an itch at the center of his back, just out of reach of his fingers. Had the song been on one of the 78s that had burned up in the fire?

"Lucky you," Perry finally said. "I mean that. Boredom is bad, but depression? It's like quicksand. You know you're getting pulled under, you know it's gonna eat you alive, and yet there's nothing you can do, Jimmy. Not a goddamn thing."

Jimmy swallowed. He *did* know that feeling but decided not to mention it.

"And then one day," Perry said, "you see this bank."

Jimmy nodded. He was looking right at it.

"And you realize that the one security guard, the *only* security guard, is fat and lazy and that the tellers are young and inexperienced, and you just happen to know the cop who drives this route, he's an old army buddy, and you know his schedule because you've ridden along with him to shoot the bull. You've had lunch with him. You know where he parks to nap. You know all this, but you don't realize you know all this until one day you're standing in line to cash a check, and it all falls into place. It's as though someone just walks up to you with a blueprint, and when you unroll it you see that it's a blueprint of your own brain—what you've been thinking, even when you don't *realize* you've been thinking. And let me tell you, Jimmy, it's like standing face to face with God himself. Yes, sir."

Jimmy heard what sounded like Perry spitting something from the tip of his tongue. Tobacco, maybe? It was a sound his father sometimes made, too. And then he heard the receiver being set into the cradle, the line going dead.

Jimmy felt a shiver run through him as he stared at the bank, and then another shiver, and another, until his teeth started to clack. When he stood up, Perry stood too, and together the boy and the dog made their way home, where a plate of food for Jimmy was growing cold.

•

"When are you going to get me another present, Jimmy? Hm?"

They were sitting in a park, surrounded by pigeons. Jimmy had brought a loaf of bread to feed them. He lowered the crime novel he'd been reading, an old pulp detective story, and there sat bored and restless Lisa Muldoon.

"What other present?"

"The dollhouse."

"What dollhouse?"

"See? Now you're just teasing me." She sighed dramatically but then she smiled. "Kiss me, Jimmy. Please? Kiss me?"

"I'll kiss you later. I'm reading."

"No. Kiss me now."

"Okay, okay," Jimmy said. "Okay, okay, okay."

Jimmy leaned over and kissed Lisa Muldoon in such a way that the brim of his fedora cast a shadow over her lips.

His lips touching hers, Jimmy thought, *I gotta think, see? I gotta be smart.* He leaned back and took a good look at Lisa Muldoon. He had to admit, she really was something. *Don't go all jingle-brained now, Jimmy,* Jimmy told himself. *Stay focused. Keep it together.*

•

Jimmy didn't have a good excuse to visit East River Savings and Loan, but he really wanted to get inside Perry's head to see what Perry saw, so he gathered up all the spare change his father kept in a purple Crown Royal bag and then the change his mother kept inside a leg of panty hose that had been scissored off from its other leg. Jimmy cinched the Crown Royal bag and tied off the pantyhose, and while waiting for Perry's next call, he took both bags, such as they were, to East River Savings and Loan, and he asked the teller if he could exchange them for dollar bills.

"We got a machine over there. Charges you 7 percent if you don't have an account with us, 4 percent if you do." Her name was Doris, according to her nameplate, and she had to lean forward to get a good view of Jimmy.

"Thank you, ma'am," Jimmy said.

He carried the coins to the machine. The ones that were in the pantyhose bounced up and down like a yo-yo when he walked. The security guard's eyes moved from Jimmy's head down to the bouncing pantyhose and then back to his head.

"I like your hat and shoes," he said.

Jimmy said, "Thank you. I'd shake your paw, but . . ." He motioned with his chin toward the coins.

He poured the coins from the Crown Royal bag into the machine first and then he untied the pantyhose and lifted it with both hands, dumping its contents into the bin carefully so as not to drop any. As he stood there listening to the machine chew the coins, his cell phone rang. He had changed the ringtone to sound like an old rotary phone, and everyone in the bank, including the security guard, turned to look at him.

"Hello?" Jimmy said, keeping his voice low.

"Why are you whispering?" Perry asked. "Where are you?"

Jimmy looked around. The security guard was still eyeing him. "I'm inside the bank," Jimmy said.

"What bank?" Perry asked. "*My* bank?"

"Yes, sir."

Perry said, "Are you nuts? Get out of there."

"But . . ."

"Right now," Perry said. "I mean it."

Jimmy turned around and headed for the door, but the security guard put a hand on his shoulder and said, "Where you going, kid?"

"Keep walking," Perry said into Jimmy's ear.

"I'll be back," Jimmy said to the guard and smiled to reassure him, but once outside Jimmy took off running. He hadn't brought Perry the dog or his bike today because of the heavy coins, but now he worried that his legs wouldn't be fast enough. The Florsheim shoes, which had been razoring into his heels despite the winter socks, weren't helping matters.

But when Jimmy glanced over his shoulder, no one was following him. No one was even looking out the bank's front doors. No one cared.

"Listen, Jimmy," Perry said. "You know where the state prison is?"

Jimmy, catching his breath, grunted.

"I want you to go there tomorrow," Perry said. "At three."

The prison was on the outskirts of the city. His family drove by it whenever they went camping. It was a lot farther away than a mere bike ride.

"You still with me here, buddy?" Perry asked.

"Yep. Still with you," Jimmy said, only this time it was Jimmy and not Perry who hung up first. Jimmy knew he'd have to take a bus to get there. And he knew what he'd have to do to be able to afford the ticket.

"You're back!" the security guard said as soon as Jimmy stepped inside the bank.

The teller said, "We were so worried about you."

The security guard laughed and said, "Women." He patted Jimmy's back and said, "Such worrywarts," then nudged Jimmy forward, where Doris counted out twenty-eight dollars and some odd change.

Jimmy folded the bills, stuck them in his pocket, and tipped his hat at the teller.

The woman said, "Goodbye, Beau Brummell," and the security guard slapped Jimmy's back on his way out.

•

The bus ride was long, hot, and crowded. Jimmy tried reading more of the old pulp novel, but he couldn't concentrate. The majority of the people on the bus—women, mostly—were getting off at the penitentiary, but the bus driver put his hand up to block Jimmy.

"You sure this is your stop?" he asked.

Jimmy nodded. "Visiting Gramps," he said.

"That's tough, kiddo." The driver sighed. "Okay, then." He lowered his arm.

As was his custom, Jimmy crossed to the opposite side of the street from wherever Perry had sent him so as to take in the whole of what Perry would be talking about. Normally he sat on the curb, but since the penitentiary was on a busy highway, Jimmy was afraid someone might run over his legs, so he sat against a rusted chain-link fence that surrounded an abandoned factory.

When the phone rang and Jimmy clicked on, Perry began talking before Jimmy could even say hello.

"What you're looking at," Perry said, "was my home for the next fifty years. Fifty years, four months, and three days. Until I got transferred to where I am now." Perry lit a cigarette. Inhaled. Exhaled. "You may be wondering how a man gets fifty-plus years for armed robbery. Well, it wasn't *just* armed robbery. There were complications at the bank. Someone did something they shouldn't have, and then I did something I shouldn't have. Are you following this?"

"I guess so. I mean, yes, sir."

"The sentence was longer, actually," Perry said. "Do you know what a compassionate release is, Jimmy? I wear an ankle bracelet now. I live in a nursing home. Want to know what's next for me? Where I go after this? The end of the line, Jimmy. Do you know what a hospice is?" Perry sighed. "Well, I never told the bastards where the money was. Any of it."

"How much was it?" Jimmy asked.

"A million seven," Perry said. "You ever wonder how much money is hidden out there in the world, Jimmy? You ever wonder how many people die without ever telling anyone where it's at?"

Jimmy stared at the penitentiary. He wasn't positive, but he thought maybe a man with a rifle in the tower was staring at him through binoculars.

"Listen, kiddo," Perry said. "I'm on my last cigarette."

"You want more?"

"No," Perry said. "This is it. The last one. I'm going to hang up and enjoy this one. But remember how I told you there'd be a surprise for you at the end?"

"Yes?"

"You got a pen to write this down, Jimmy? Because have I got a surprise for you!"

The guard in the tower lowered his binoculars and turned away. Jimmy took a deep breath and held it as long as he could, feverishly writing as Perry gave him directions for where he could find his big surprise.

"When should I go there?" Jimmy asked.

"Tomorrow. Five p.m., sharp. Got it?"

"Got it."

•

Jimmy must have misread the bus schedule because the next bus didn't pick him up until mid-evening and didn't drop him off downtown until almost eight o'clock at night. And then there was the long walk home. He was supposed to have been home for dinner at six o'clock. No matter how he looked at it, he didn't see a good outcome. But why should he care? He knew what Perry's surprise was. He knew it as well as he knew when Perry the dog was hungry or when Perry the dog needed to go outside to do his business. Jimmy *knew*. The old man was dying, and he was leading Jimmy to a secret location where the money was hidden. One million and seven hundred thousand dollars! The directions were written in his book's backflap.

Back home, Jimmy opened the door slowly, hoping the squeaking hinges wouldn't call attention to him, but it was too late. His mother and father were already sitting so that they both faced the door, waiting for Jimmy to step inside.

Jimmy's father stood up and moved toward him. He said, "And just where the hell have you been?"

Jimmy didn't answer. He looked to his mother for help, but his mother looked as angry as his father.

"Answer me," his father said.

"I don't understand," his mother said. "We bought you that new phone. You could have called us. Why didn't you call us?"

Jimmy didn't have any answers for them. He reached down to pet Perry, whose tail slapped the furniture, but his father pushed the dog away with his foot and said, "You've got until I count to three, young man. One."

Jimmy saw it all: Perry in the bank, a gun held on the teller. The teller stuffing the money into several bags until the bags were almost too full to zip shut.

"Two."

A guard reached for his gun, and Perry, catching sight of the man in a mirror, spun around and shot the guard dead.

"Three."

"Tell *me*," Jimmy said.

"Tell you what?" his father replied.

Jimmy took a step closer. "Tell me," Jimmy said, sneering, "just what kind of a palooka smokes Virginia Slims?"

The blow happened so fast, Jimmy didn't see it coming. He was on the floor, too dizzy to stand. The paperback novel had flown from his hands. Perry the dog licked Jimmy's wounded eye, but his father was yelling for his mother to get that damn dog out of the room, to get it out *right now*. All the while, Jimmy's mother was yelling at his father for striking Jimmy. Jimmy wasn't crying, but he could feel his face swelling around his right eye, puffing up like a balloon beginning to inflate.

"Goddamn it!" his father said and left the house.

"Here," his mother said, but when she reached for him, Jimmy flinched. "I just want to take a look," his mother said. And then she peeled Jimmy's hands away from his face. "For the love of God," she said at the sight of him. "Wait here. I'm going to get some ice to put on it."

Perry stayed beside Jimmy, anxiously swiping his tail, the two of them waiting until Jimmy's mother returned with some ice wrapped in a dish towel. She gave it to Jimmy, and he held it against his eye.

"We don't even recognize you anymore, Jimmy," his mother said. "Why are you using all these strange words? Palooka? The other day you asked me for a sawbuck and a fin? Who are you?"

"I'm who I've always been," Jimmy said. "I'm me."

At that, Jimmy's mother's eyes turned wet. She raised her chin and took a deep breath through her nose, then wiped her eyes with the back of her arm.

"Well, all right, you're you," she said. Her hands were shaking. "I don't know what that means, but . . . okay."

Jimmy knew he should comfort her—he knew that would be the right thing to do—but he didn't. They would all know soon enough what he meant and who he was when he came home with duffel bags stuffed full of money.

His mother sighed and stood. "I don't know what to do anymore. I really don't, Jimmy."

•

The next day, with his eye purple and black, he called Lisa Muldoon and told her where to meet him, and then he took Perry the dog outside without anyone noticing that he was leaving. Jimmy put on his mother's sunglasses, swung a leg over his bike, and pedaled away, Perry jogging on a leash alongside him.

Lisa Muldoon was already waiting at the designated corner for him, but she was staring at her shoes. "Kiss me?" she asked gloomily, moving only her eyes to look up at Jimmy, but when he took off his mother's sunglasses, she gasped then moved toward him, holding her finger close to his eye but not touching it. "What—?"

"Shhhh," Jimmy said. "We're running late."

"I want you to tell me what happened," Lisa said. She reached up and touched around her own eye, the one that mirrored his, as though this might offer a clue.

"Please," Jimmy said. "I'll tell you later, tomato. I promise."

Jimmy wasn't sure how many trips he and Lisa Muldoon would have to make to retrieve all the money. Could they do it all in one trip? Would it take all week? Jimmy had already planned on stashing it in the far, dark corners of the attic until he could come up with a better place to stow it. It was possible, of course, that Perry was just some old loon or a hophead, or maybe Perry was hoping to use Jimmy to chisel his parents out of their life savings. Maybe it was all part of a long con job. But Perry's stories were too convincing not to see this journey through to its end.

As per Perry's plan, Jimmy and Lisa, with Perry the dog in tow, arrived at the shopping mall. Before it was a mall, it had been a factory for the Ford Motor Company. Before that, it had been a factory for airplane motors during World War II. Because of its peculiar history, the mall was a compound of many buildings and outposts, all connected by an underground tunnel of boutique stores and mall offices. But there were also mysterious doors and hallways that led who knew where. It was the stuff of urban legend that everyone in the neighborhood grew up hearing about. Rumor was that there were other tunnels, a network of them, and that some of those led all the way to the airport three miles north of the mall.

Jimmy locked up his bike then led Lisa Muldoon and Perry the dog down a set of stairs that opened onto a group of stores. Closely following the directions Perry had given him, Jimmy took them into a corridor that wound past mall offices and restrooms, and then he opened a door labeled B-207. It was a boiler room.

Jimmy, Lisa Muldoon, and Perry the dog made their way through the hissing, clanking, and grinding room until they reached an unmarked door. Jimmy creaked open that door, exposing an even darker room. It was dank and smelled like mold. He used his phone's flashlight. Every fifty yards or so hung a dim or burnt-out lightbulb. Otherwise, there was only darkness and the sound of dripping water.

"You're never going to kiss me again, are you?" Lisa Muldoon said.

"Can we talk about this later? Now's not a good time."

"When are you going to give me that dollhouse?"

"What dollhouse?"

"The one that's twelve feet high."

"I don't even know what you're talking about."

Jimmy counted off footsteps. The air, metallic and dusty, was hard to breathe. He sliced away cobwebs with his free arm. When he reached three hundred and fifty steps, he turned left and walked four hundred and twenty-seven more. And then he stopped. Exactly as Perry had predicted, Jimmy was now standing directly under a bulb that burned brighter than any of the others, as though someone had purposely screwed in a bulb with a higher wattage.

Jimmy shined the flashlight all around, looking for bags full of dough. Above him were steel beams, where stacks of cash could be tucked, but Jimmy didn't see any up there. What if someone had taken the money? What if the money had been found years ago without Perry even knowing it?

A voice erupted from the dark: "Jimmy Presko? Is that you, boy?"

Jimmy spun around. In a white terrycloth robe, a fedora, and a pair of brown loafers stood a gaunt old man. The old man smiled. "Surprise!" But then he narrowed his eyes at Perry the dog, and he looked up at Lisa Muldoon, who was brushing her flapper's haircut with her fingers. Jimmy reached up and adjusted his own fedora, confused, until he saw the old man smiling again, his eyes filling with tears.

To the dog, Perry said, "You're so . . . *small.*"

Jimmy let go of the miniature American Eskimo's leash, and Perry dropped to his knees to greet the dog, who licked his face as though the two were old companions reunited. Perry's robe opened enough to reveal his shriveled body, and Jimmy wished he'd brought a coat to cover up the old man. Jimmy took hold of Lisa's hand and squeezed it, but she did not return the squeeze. *It's over*, he thought, and he felt an actual pain of regret in his chest, and then he heard his own breath leave his mouth.

Several beams of light crisscrossed the ceiling and walls until they landed on Perry and Perry the dog. Perry's arms were draped around the dog's neck, and his forehead rested against its head.

"There he is!" someone yelled.

A group of men materialized out of the dark, one of them a security guard, the others dressed in scrubs.

"Perry!" the guard called out, and the dog moaned, swiping its tail. "Perry, Perry, Perry," the guard said upon approaching, and the dog moaned louder.

A light fell on Jimmy and Lisa, who squinted and ducked their heads from the intense glare. "Are you okay?" The guard stepped closer and took Jimmy's chin in his hand, examining his eye. "Did Perry do this to you?"

"No, sir."

"You sure?"

"Yes, sir."

"Well, you better come along with us. We've got a lot to sort out." He turned the flashlight toward Perry again and said, "You make me earn my money. I'll give you that much, old man."

Ignoring the guard, Perry remained on the ground with Perry. Perry whispered into Perry's ear, "You're such a good boy. Yes you are. Yes you are."

•

The group of men led Perry, Jimmy, Lisa, and Perry the dog through a labyrinth of tunnels and corridors until they reached a door that opened up into a clean, bright basement. From there, they took an elevator up three floors. The elevator door slid open, and a wave of antiseptic air and fluorescent lights hit them as nurses walked briskly by and a man with a walker stopped, peered inside the elevator, and said, "Hello, Perry, I see they caught you again," and then kept going.

As they exited the elevator, Lisa whispered, "So it's true what everyone says about the underground tunnels."

"It's true," Jimmy answered. "It's all true."

The debriefing took place in a conference room and lasted longer than Jimmy could have imagined. Parents were called. The police came—real police—to ask questions. Nobody looked happy. Jimmy knew without having to be told that it was over between him and Lisa Muldoon. He suspected that his parents would never let him out of the house after this incident. But worst of all was that they were telling him he wouldn't be allowed to talk to Perry, the old man, ever again.

"He has stage 4 prostate cancer," a doctor told Jimmy while his parents sat like guards on either side of him. "He'll be lucky if he has another month. In all likelihood, he'll go to a hospice next week."

A policeman said, "He lied on his 'Grandpa, Please!' application. Felons aren't eligible to participate. That should go without saying. It's a new program. A good program. I'm sure they're still ironing out the glitches."

"Glitches?" his mother asked. "Is that what they're calling this? A *glitch?*"

His father wagged his head. If he were a cartoon father in an old cartoon, steam would have been blowing out of his ears.

Through a plate-glass window, Jimmy could see two attendants walking Perry down a hallway, probably to his room. He expected the old man to turn around and give Jimmy a thumbs up, but Perry shuffled into the room without looking back.

Instead of crying, which was what he wanted to do, Jimmy started humming "You Are My Sunshine." It was the song that Perry had hummed before, the one that Jimmy hadn't been able to remember, but he remembered it now and could have belted out the lyrics, but he didn't. He just hummed it quietly to himself until they were done with the debriefing.

•

In the nursing home's parking lot, Jimmy and Perry the dog stood at a distance while his mother and father argued.

"Fine," he heard his father say. "I'll stay in a motel tonight, if that's how you want it." And then, "No, no, no. I'll take a cab. Hell, I'll *walk* if I have to."

On the ride home, Jimmy sat in the backseat with his arm slung over Perry the dog's neck while his mother drove. He could see in the rearview mirror his father standing in the parking lot, watching them leave. The further they drove, the smaller he became, until he wasn't in the mirror at all.

After picking up Jimmy's bike at the mall, his mother drove toward home without any more detours, passing several locations where Jimmy had been sent by Perry. When they passed East River Savings and Loan, Jimmy shivered. *The money is still out there somewhere*, he thought. *Over a million dollars.*

The way Jimmy saw it, he had a month to break the old man out of the hospice. Less than a month, truth be told. He could take the old man to Havana Lounge and Cigar, where, after a few drinks and a smoke, the old man might remember where the money was. And then Jimmy could win back the love of the only girl he had ever kissed. He could go to her house with a box of chocolates, lift the lid to show her, and tell her that there was more where that came from.

But Jimmy already knew, as well as he knew that Perry the dog was sitting next to him, that Lisa Muldoon would shut the door between them. He knew that his pleas would come too late. Jimmy was damaged goods now. A bad seed.

I didn't want to believe it was really over, he imagined himself saying many years from now, in a phone call to a boy his own age. *I couldn't fathom that she wouldn't speak to me again, not after all we'd gone through.* And then he would hang up on the boy, finish his cigarette, and try to remember all the glorious things that had come into his life, all the glorious things he'd ever lost. *What a life*, Jimmy Presko thought in the backseat of his parents' car. What a strange and thrilling and heartbreaking life!

THE NEXT MORNING

This was ten years ago. Alexis, my wife, had moved out the week before. We had separated but agreed we could see other people, and I had talked a woman named June into coming back to my house with me. I'd met June earlier that night in a bar called The Next Morning, a cheery, optimistic name for a shithole of a place, but the jukebox was good, and the patrons were generous when it came to buying shots for everyone huddled together at the short end of the bar. June stood out from the other women at The Next Morning in that she wore a dress instead of jeans and a T-shirt, and she had a string of pearls around her neck. They looked real, too.

June had said, "You look sad," and I said, "I was thinking how much money I'd save drinking at home," and then a few hours later we were mixing drinks in my kitchen. I sliced limes, and she hammered the ice with a meat tenderizer. We listened to albums—Sam Cooke, Wilson Pickett, Aretha Franklin—and I would occasionally say things like, "Goddamn, listen to that note she hit" or "Wilson Pickett . . . best soul screamer, hands down," and June, holding the drink above her head the way Lady Liberty holds the torch, would close her eyes and sway her hips, or she'd try to lure my cat Willie toward her, inexplicably calling him Bubba. "Here, Bubba-Bubba. Here, Bubba." Willie was five years old and black with long hair and piercing eyes—a spry and curious rescue.

After one of my trips to the bathroom, I found June in the hallway, holding the trapdoor in the floor open, and peering down into the darkness. The house had no basement, so the trapdoor opened up to the plumbing and the ground beneath the house.

June looked up, still holding a drink in one hand, and said, "I opened it to see what was inside."

"And?" I said.

"And your cat ran out."

"Willie?" I said.

June looked like she was going to cry.

"It's okay," I said. "He'll come back."

"Do you let him outside?"

"No," I said. "Never." When June crouched to peer down into the darkness again, I walked over beside her. "It's okay," I said. "I'll put some food out. Here," I said, helping June up and taking control of the trapdoor's handle. "I'll leave the hole open. It'll be fine."

After another two drinks, June seemed to have forgotten about Willie. Every few songs, she would light up and scream, "Motherfuckers!" and I'd laugh. I kept bringing our glasses back to the kitchen for refills, dumping the murky fruit slices into the sink and filling us back up again, bringing shots at least twice—*one for you, one for me*—until the final drink where we ended up side by side in the kitchen together.

"No music," she said and pouted.

"Oh, shit," I said, listening to the silence coming from the other room. And then I told her a story about a time when I was so drunk, I leaned against a dead tree to take a whiz and the dead tree started to tip over. I quickly grabbed onto the tree, clutching it for the incomprehensible reason drunk people do the things they do, and when the tree fell, I bounced off it and rolled into a marshy bog of some sort. June wasn't listening, I realized. She was poking the fruit rinds into the garbage disposal with a wooden stirring spoon. I saw a mosquito flying near my head—and I thought, irrationally, that my wife had released a box full of mosquitoes in the house to foil any chance I had of getting laid that night. I swatted at the mosquito and missed, and when I couldn't see it again, I reached behind me and flipped on the garbage disposal.

At first, I wasn't sure what was happening. June let out what I had thought was a Wilson Pickett soul scream, but the proximity of the sound caused a ghost-chill to rip through me. The disposal sounded like it was broken, and June screamed again. When I turned and saw blood and flesh spraying from the drain, I realized (slowly) that June had put the wooden spoon aside and had stuck her arm down the drain to get rid of the remaining rinds. It may have been only a second before I turned the disposal off, but it felt like a minute had passed. The sight had frozen me in place. I expected June to pull her hand from the drain the moment the grinding stopped, and I prayed that any injury she sustained was something that could be taken care of with a Band-Aid, but when she didn't remove her hand, I wondered if maybe it had gotten stuck. I taught second and third grades. Kids were always getting body parts stuck in odd places. Heads between wrought iron bars. Hands in jars.

"Oh my God," I said when I pulled her arm free. "Oh my God. Oh my fucking God."

Most of her hand was gone. When she saw what had become of her hand along with the amount of blood she was losing, she collapsed—first to her knees and then, like a limbo dancer, backwards, her calves still tucked under her. I was certain she would die there on my floor—I had never seen so much blood—but the paramedics, whom I had somehow managed to call, were able to save her. Her hand, however—most of it still stuck in the pipes underneath my sink—would be beyond repair. A surgeon would tell me this later after nudging me on the couch in an emergency room, where I awoke in a drunk fog, unsure at what point in my life I was stepping into. I could have been any age, anywhere, hearing news of anyone in my life. I listened; I nodded; and then I called for a cab to take me back home.

•

I never told Alexis what had happened that night. From what little research I did the next few months, I discovered that June was married to a man in the oil business in Lafayette, Louisiana, where we lived. Nearly everyone I met was in the oil business in some capacity, and the money was often good. June's husband, a man named David LaFage, was CEO of a company that handled underground property rights. Whatever her reasons—and I could imagine there were many—June never contacted me about what had happened. A few months later, after I had sobered up, after I had replaced the pipes under the sink with new pipes, Alexis and I decided to give our marriage another try.

One afternoon, several months after we'd gotten back together, Alexis said, "So. Tell me again what happened to Willie?"

"He ran out when I was coming in with groceries," I said. Every night since his disappearance, I had left the trapdoor open in case Willie returned, but with each passing day, my hope deflated ever so slightly.

"Hm," Alexis said. "That's odd. He would run whenever I opened the door."

"It's weird," I said. "I know."

Alexis kept her eyes on me. She said, "Did you date anyone when we were apart?"

Heat rose to my face, and I could tell that Alexis was watching closely for signs of dishonesty, but I said, "No. You?"

Alexis narrowed her eyes. She said, "You're not telling me the truth."

"Of course I'm telling you the truth."

Alexis was a pharmacist. She offered consultations to people who kept hidden from her the origins of their ailments, but she could see embarrassment and shame in their eyes. She'd often told me about the ways in which they'd tell her, with nothing more than a look, secrets that their hearts would never reveal.

"What?" I said. "I mean, I met someone once. She came over for drinks."

"She came *here?*" Alexis asked, and I immediately regretted admitting anything. I had foolishly thought a half-truth could save me.

"Yeah. For drinks. That's all."

"Hm," Alexis said, sizing me up. "Did you use our bed?"

"For *drinks*," I repeated. "She came here for *drinks*."

"I just find it curious, is all," Alexis said.

"What do you find curious?"

"That you came back here. Just for drinks."

"We listened to some albums, too," I said. "Okay?"

"Oh. See? You didn't say that. I thought it was *just drinks*."

"Are we really having this conversation?" I asked. "Look, I don't care if you dated anyone. I don't care what you may or may not have done or where you did it or didn't do it."

Alexis nodded, but she kept watching me.

"What albums did you listen to?" she asked.

"I don't know. Wilson Pickett. Aretha Franklin. Another one, I think?"

"Did you tell her that Wilson Pickett was hands down the best soul screamer?"

"Why? What if I did?"

Alexis shook her head, as if to say, *no reason*.

"What?" I said. "Is that something I always say? Am I that predictable?"

"I don't know," she said. "You said that to me the first night we slept together."

"Oh, *really*," I said, and I wanted to ask her if I had also chopped off most of her hand by accident that night, too, but I stood and walked away. I got in my car and drove. Marriage, I was coming to realize, was a long stretch of domestic chores punctuated by bursts of aimless driving. It was possible other couples had it better—witty banter, spontaneous vacations, acrobatic sex that left their hearts pounding while the bedsheets absorbed their sweat. In my marriage, something had happened—I wasn't sure what—that had left Alexis wanting to believe the worst in me.

But for the life of me, I wasn't sure when or why the scales had tipped out of my favor, only that they had. And I had no idea how to tip them back.

•

Five years after the night with June, Alexis and I went to the nicest restaurant in town to celebrate Alexis's promotion. It was a restaurant that required me to examine myself in the mirror before we went inside to make sure that there wasn't a stray hair growing out of my forehead, that my face was relatively clean, and that my beard and mustache were trimmed in such a way that no whiskers were curling up into a nostril, as they sometimes did.

"You clean up nicely," Alexis said when I stepped out into the living room.

"As do you," I said. She was wearing a crushed velvet dress and had placed a flower in her hair. Where she had acquired the flower, I couldn't have said. Before we left, I propped open the trapdoor. It had become as involuntary as making sure the stove was off and the doors were all locked.

At the restaurant, every item on the menu contained ingredients that I didn't recognize, and I had to ask the waiter, a tall fellow with slicked-back hair and tattoos creeping out from the sleeves of his shirt, what several of the words meant. The menu exhausted me. But I played along, asking questions neither I nor the waiter wanted to hear.

"It's just a sauce," he said about the last word I had quizzed him on.

"A sauce. Nice," I said. "I'll take that. But without the sauce."

"Very good then," the waiter said and left us alone.

"So!" I said to Alexis. "To the job!" I lifted my glass of wine and clanked it against her glass, also of wine, and I started to sip when a man approached our table.

"Alexis?" he said.

Alexis, still smiling, looked up at the approaching man, but when she saw who he was, she quit smiling and cocked her head, the way a dog might when trouble is near.

"It's Sam," he said. "We . . ." He looked over at me, assessed the situation. "We met many years ago."

I knew Alexis well enough to know that she knew full well who this man was, but for whatever the reason, she wanted to remain coy.

"Anyway," Sam said. "It was at least four years ago. Maybe longer. I saw you just now and thought, how strange to live in the same town with someone you meet once and then never see again."

"It is strange," Alexis said. "I'm sorry I don't remember you."

Sam said, "What can I say? I'm not very memorable, I guess." Sam looked at me and, conspiratorially, said, "Be careful, buddy. She may not remember *you* in four years."

He bent forward, rapped his knuckles on the table three times, as though it were a door, then stood up straight, smiled, and walked away.

"Who the hell was that?" I asked.

"I don't know," Alexis said. "I have no idea."

"I think you know him," I said.

Alexis picked up her empty wine glass, finished the final couple of drops, set it down. She said, "Really. Is there something about me that you know that I don't?"

"It's just the way you looked at him when he approached," I said. "I've known you a long time, okay? I can read you."

"What am I thinking now?" she asked.

I said, "You're thinking about bringing home some arsenic from the pharmacy and poisoning me with it."

"We don't carry arsenic at CVS," she said.

"Too bad," I said.

When the waiter came over to see if everything was okay, I told him it was, but I suspected he and the other waitstaff had been watching us from a distance. He nodded, retreated.

I said, "I'm sorry. I don't care if you know him or not. I just don't understand why . . ." Before I could finish my sentence, Alexis had stood and walked away. I'd thought she had gone to the restroom, but after fifteen minutes I had another thought. I walked to the exit and saw that my car was still there. I asked the hostess if she'd seen a woman about yea tall leave in a huff. The hostess confirmed that, yes, a woman did leave abruptly.

"Great," I said.

I called her cell, but it went straight to voicemail.

"Alexis," I said, trying to keep my voice down. "Call me back, okay?"

I returned to my table and began to eat my steak, which had arrived. I knew she would have walked all three miles home through some sketchy neighborhoods, just to spite me. And I knew it would only be worse if I went looking for her. I ordered dessert, a crème brûlée, and took my time eating it, tapping the caramelized sugar lightly with my spoon before each bite, the way guests at a wedding tap the sides of a glass to initiate a speech.

"Check, please!" I called out, and within fifteen minutes I was at The Next Morning, drinking vodka tonics. I hadn't been there since that night with June—had been afraid people would remember seeing me leave with her that night only to see her next time maimed and haunted, but no one cared when I walked in.

"Why The Next Morning? What's the import of that?" I asked the bartender. She had a lip ring and purple hair, and her eyes went out of focus at my question, as though I had just tried the lamest pickup line she'd ever heard.

"Welp," she said. "Better than The Morning After. The Morning After sounds like a bar that provides abortions."

I thought about the pieces of June's hands still in my drain when I got home that next day and about how it had taken three trips to Lowe's to get all the parts I needed to replace the pipes. I had felt like a criminal, flushing out the pieces of flesh and bone into the tub and then tossing it all in a Hefty sack on top of God only knew what—spaghetti from the day before, likely, and a mound of damp coffee grounds. But what was I supposed to do? Put it in a Ziploc bag and rush it to the hospital? Mail it to her?

The bartender announced last call, and I said, "The Morning After. There was a song called 'The Morning After.' It was the theme to *The Poseidon Adventure*."

"Dude," the bartender said. "Don't."

"What?" I asked.

"Just don't," she said.

•

Ten years after the night with June, I was helping Alexis load the moving truck she had rented. She had rented one that was too small for the amount of stuff she owned, so we had to make multiple trips from our house to her new place across town. The truck burned oil, and with each trip there and back, people would slow down to stare inside the truck's cab to see what kind of heinous person would pollute the environment the way I was doing.

Alexis's new house was on a hill, and I offered, perhaps foolishly, to help her with all her boxes. She was a reader of thick hardcover books, and her library took up a good fifty boxes in the truck. For each trip up the hill, I would pile four boxes onto the two-wheel hand truck, and then I would pull it over the street's curb and start hauling it up the hill until I reached the brick steps, which required pulling the truck with both hands, grunting, trying not to trip, pulling again, trying not to let go of the handle.

"You should rest," Alexis said. "Drink some water."

"Nah."

And down I'd go again. By the fifth trip, my right knee had begun to ache. By the tenth, it felt like a balloon filled with gasoline and set on fire.

Alexis said, "You should stop."

"Nah," I said. I needed to make only a few more trips up and down the hill. Why would I stop? Up I went, until there were tears in my eyes. "Jesus," I said. "Jesus Christ."

The last load was Sisyphean, stopping and starting, gaining and then losing ground. My knee felt as large and fiery as the sun, the rest of my body as useless and unappealing as space garbage.

Later that week, after Alexis was settled in her new place, I went to an orthopedist and had my knee looked at.

"Torn meniscus," the doctor told me after twisting it once and listening to me howl.

"Do I need an MRI?" I asked. "How do you know?"

"What do you do for a living?"

"I teach grade school."

"Okay then," the doctor said, perking up. "If you see a boy with a big wet spot on his crotch, do you know what happened?" He smiled.

I said nothing.

The doctor said, "Let's get you scheduled for a surgery. I do these all day long on Tuesdays and Thursdays. Takes less than an hour. Two tiny holes in your knee is all I need. You'll be in and out of there before you know it." He clapped my back and said, "It's possible the boy spilled soda on himself, but this? It's a torn meniscus."

One week later, I was standing at the check-in counter at the hospital with my cab driver. I was informed by the hospital that I was to bring someone with me, but I didn't know anyone who could make it, so I paid my cab driver twenty bucks extra to pretend he was my friend. He was from Zimbabwe, and I could barely understand his English, but he understood me perfectly well.

I said to the woman behind the counter, "This is my friend, Tawonga Chakwana."

Tawonga, scrolling through Facebook on his phone, nodded.

I said, "He's got to run an errand while I'm in surgery, but he'll be back."

Tawonga, still scrolling, nodded again. The woman behind the counter didn't even look up at us. She said, "You need to fill out these forms, front and back, and I'll need your insurance card and a driver's license."

Tawonga and I shook hands, and he left me alone. I took the clipboard and pen and then limped over to a sofa. There was a message on my phone from Alexis. She wondered if I knew the best way to open a window that had been sealed shut with layers of paint. She wondered if she could borrow my toolbox. She wondered how she could breathe if the house she was living in couldn't. I hadn't told Alexis about my surgery. The way I saw it, all my problems were now my problems and my problems alone.

Two hours later I was in the operating room, giving in to the anesthesia, when I tried to say "My knee has been a wreck for a while now" but said instead "My life has been a wreck for a while now" and was pretty certain the doctor responded, "We'll get it fixed up by the time the big hand reaches nine," and I said, "Really? You will?" And then I didn't remember anything else until I woke up in the recovery room, eventually got help putting on my clothes, and then waited sleepily in a lounge for Tawonga to come get me, a lounge full of other patients' family members, but Tawonga was nowhere to be seen.

I was not allowed to leave the room alone for reasons having to do with insurance, so I would fall asleep in my chair, wake up, moan because of my sore knee, and then say, "I'm going to kill you, Tawonga. If it's the last thing I do."

"Excuse me," a woman said after the room had thinned, the sky beyond the thick plate-glass windows clouding. She was sitting in a chair behind me, and she had to twist her torso to see me as I had to twist mine to see her.

"Do you need a ride?" she asked.

"I do," I said. "But you're here, too."

"I'm a guest," she said. "My ex-husband's sister is here, but I was just told that she's going to be another two hours."

"Oh," I said. "Is she okay?"

"Yeah, yeah," the woman said. "But it'll be two hours before she's ready."

She walked over to the receptionist to explain the new arrangement, and then we had to wait for a nurse to find a wheelchair to wheel me outside while my new friend drove her car to the curb. Apparently, once you set foot inside someone's car, you're no longer the responsibility of the hospital. You're on your own. You're free. The nurse tossed my crutches into the car's back seat, and I eased myself out of the wheelchair, hopping on my good foot and then collapsing into the bucket seat. The nurse shut the door once my gimpy leg was out of harm's way.

"Oh, man," I said. "Thank you."

And that's when I noticed the woman's hand resting on the steering wheel. It wasn't a complete hand. It was a partial hand.

I didn't say anything and neither did she except to say that she got my address from the receptionist. I tried staying awake, but I must have dozed off for a bit. When I opened my eyes, we were passing The Next Morning, long boarded up and vacant for serving underage drinkers too many times. When she pulled up to my house, I told her that I really appreciated her kindness, and then I opened the door to begin the treacherous journey of using crutches for the first time.

After I pulled the crutches free but before I could shut the back door, June said, "I never blamed you, you know."

I nodded.

"I appreciate that," I said.

"I wouldn't say what you went through was worse," she said, "but it couldn't have been easy."

"There's no comparison," I said.

She nodded, and I shut the door. I was so tired, I wasn't sure I could make it the few steps it required to reach my house without taking a nap. I had never been so tired in my life. Slowly, I made my way up the sidewalk to my house, planting the crutches and then swinging myself forward, planting and swinging, over and over, until I reached the front door.

I swung myself inside, bouncing off one wall and almost falling into another. I remembered that Alexis had sent me a text, but I couldn't remember the point of it, only that the house needed to breathe. I felt it, too—the lack of oxygen, the walls trying to suck in air through its dark vents. I opened over a dozen windows and removed their screens to let in even more air, all the while hopping on one foot. Is this what Alexis had meant for me to do? In the hallway, the trapdoor was propped up, as it had been for the past ten years, but I removed it altogether from the floor and leaned it up against the wall, and the whoosh of air was as though duct tape had been removed from the mouth of a hostage.

In the living room, I set aside the crutches and fell back onto the couch. Almost instantly, I fell into the deep sleep of lingering anesthesia— three, four hours without moving—and when I woke up, the house was dark, but I could sense someone was in the room with me. I leaned over and turned on the end-table lamp, and two dozen animals momentarily froze, like burglars at an unanticipated noise, before resuming their activities. There were at least three unfamiliar cats, a squirrel, and a hunched chipmunk. Two birds wheeled past me. It was as though every animal that Willie had spied through the windows, every animal he had chased despite the glass between them, every animal that had tormented him by their mere presence—they had all come to pay their respects for the old cat that had never returned home. I wiped my eyes, sad and knee-sore patron saint of wild beasts that I hoped to be. When my knee felt better, I would dig a hole and bury Willie's rusting bowls and cobwebbed toys, but right now, more than anything, I needed sleep. Another hour or two. Maybe longer. I curled up on the couch, shivering, but nodded off at the first blush of morning, the sun's hazy promise of the new day that you could always count on—until you couldn't.

THE DEVIL IN THE DETAILS

Part One

It was the last thing on Mary Flynn's mind when she crawled into bed that night, but by the time she closed her eyes for sleep, the overwhelming lure of sin had wrapped itself around her neck, as comforting as a scarf.

The year was 1853. Mary was ten years old, a little girl in a small southern Illinois town, and each night, before blowing out the candle in her room, her father told her a story from the Bible.

"Adam named me serpent, so serpent I shall be," her father had begun tonight. "I watched Adam name every beast of the field, the cattle and the fowl, and then the next day I watched Eve form of Adam's rib, and I thought, *she's mine.*" He reached out and pinched Mary in the area of her ribs, and she squealed.

The entire time her father spoke, Mary imagined the snake speaking directly to her. Was the snake smiling? Yes. Well, sort of. All snakes smiled, more or less. But this snake was meeting Mary's eyes as it spoke and slithered closer.

Her father concluded, "And that's when I saw something in Eve I had not seen before, something that made me want to slither from a branch and onto her arm, and then slither from her arm to her breasts, and then wrap my cold flesh against her warm flesh, tightening ever so gently so as to feel her against me, the two of us one flesh, as she had been with Adam. I saw it in her eyes, how she would enjoy this, and then she reached for the fruit and plucked it from its stem."

Her father set his black cowboy hat atop his head and then put his lips close to the flame, so close Mary was certain he was going to burn them, and then he smiled and blew gently, allowing the flame to flicker and grow before he blew harder. The room went dark.

Her father, the sheriff, extinguished lives in much the same manner. He would tell a story to the gathering crowd while the criminal stood with a noose around his neck, wrists tied behind his back, and rope so tight around his ankles that the condemned man had to be carried to his final destination. A balled-up kerchief would be stuffed inside the criminal's mouth. It was too late for pleas, her father reasoned, and he certainly didn't want to be interrupted while telling the crowd a story, sometimes the same story he'd told Mary the night before—the story of Sodom and Gomorrah, or the story of Abraham giving his son Isaac back to God, or, as tonight, the story of the serpent and the Tree of Knowledge.

"Do not take advantage of a widow or an orphan," he yelled last week from the gallows, quoting from memory. "If you do and they cry out to me, I will certainly hear their cry. My anger will be aroused, and I will kill you with the sword. Your wives will become widows and your children fatherless."

He stood by the lever that opened the trapdoor, but instead of simply pulling it, he waited until the crowd had worked itself into a lather—the wronged party yelling for the lever to be pulled, the con- demned man's family begging for mercy.

At her father's request, Mary had gathered as many of her class- mates as she could find, and they called out for the sheriff to pull the lever, parroting the adults beside them. And then, finally, her father pulled the wooden stick, the floor below the criminal's bound feet opened, and the crowd fell silent as the condemned man's neck snapped. The dead man's family wailed loudly, running to the gallows before deputies could cut the body down.

The candle's been blown out, Mary thought upon seeing the dead man. Smiling, she shut her eyes.

•

Until she was ten years old, Mary held a prestigious and much-envied position among her classmates as the daughter of the town's sheriff, but then the cold wind blew and a shift occurred. Most of the adults in town remained at home during the executions, and once some of them found out that Mary had been luring their children to these displays, they openly criticized her for what she was doing.

"You're an evil little girl," they told her while other parents clutched their children closer whenever Mary appeared in the town square, as though she were capable of the most heinous acts.

Mary still had her friends, but once word circulated that she was an evil girl, it eventually penetrated her inner circle. One by one, the girls dropped away until one day Mary found herself all alone.

And then came the snake.

•

For as long as Mary could remember, she'd always walked to school with her friends, cutting through acres of woods together, following a path that had come about from years of use as a shortcut. The rest of the woods flourished, a dense patch of bizarre weeds—some poisonous to the touch—and vines that slowly strangled whatever they had seductively wrapped themselves around. There were dozens of fallen trees, leafless and gray, including one large tree lying across their path, requiring the children to climb over it each morning, risking a torn dress or skinned knee.

After rumors of Mary's wickedness took root and spread, her friends stayed several yards ahead of her, as though they didn't know her, picking up their pace even as she called out for them to slow down.

"*Please*," she whined. "I can't walk as fast as you in these shoes. *Please* slow down."

Her friends, speaking amongst themselves, acted as though they hadn't heard her. Only Rachel, the last friend that still talked to Mary, waved her arm and called out, "Hurry up, Mary! We can't wait for you!"

It was an unseasonably hot May morning. Mary attempted to cross the fallen tree, but before she could swing herself over the trunk, her left leg snagged on something. It burned, too—a searing hot pain. She attempted to detach her leg from whatever had taken hold, but her leg barely budged. The pain grew sharper, her leg hotter. When she finally looked down, she saw that a cottonmouth had sunk its fangs into her calf and wasn't letting go. It had come from the nearby Big Muddy River, no doubt, out of which snakes slithered every fall, searching for cracks and crevices where they could burrow over winter.

Mary almost fainted at the sight of the snake, but she held on long enough to shriek for help.

"A snake's got me! Please come back!"

But the girls walked faster, rounding a bend and disappearing from Mary's view. They never even looked back.

Mary slid off the tree and tried running home, hoping the snake would let go of her, but the snake held on, and Mary's progress was excruciatingly slow. She was barely able to move the leg that the snake was biting. When she looked behind her and saw that the snake was longer than she was tall, she fell to her knees. She felt as though she were swimming through the woods, each wave of bark and stone growing darker than the last, until everything turned black.

•

What Mary saw when she opened her eyes was an old man's lips pressing tightly against her bare leg. First, she screamed and tried wriggling away, but the man, keeping his lips firmly in place, looked up at her, and his eyes told the whole story: *Don't move . . . I'm saving your life.*

And this was, in fact, what he was doing. He was sucking the venom from her leg. He would suck then spit, and then he would suck some more. When he was done sucking out the venom, he stood and lifted Mary up into the air, draping her over his shoulder as though she were a sack of grain, and began walking into town. He didn't speak. He was as old as her grandfather but stronger than anyone else she knew, except for maybe her father. He picked up his pace.

"Am I going to die?" Mary asked the man carrying her.

The man didn't answer.

He carried her to Dr. Merchant's front door and kicked with his foot. The doctor himself opened the door but took a step back at the sight of the man.

"What did you do to her?" Dr. Merchant asked.

"Snake bite on the leg," the man said. "Big one." He handed the girl over and said, "I seen to sucking out the poison."

"Okay then," the doctor said. "You can go now."

The old man regarded Mary in the doctor's arms. He tried to touch Mary's head, as though to say, "You'll be all right," but the doctor stepped back and said, "Go on now. I've got work to do." The doctor carried Mary into another room. He said, "I don't know who's got more evil in him—the snake that bit you or that old man." He set Mary down atop an examination table and said, "Let's see your leg now, dear."

•

The old man, it turned out, was Phineas T. Rider. Rumor was that Phineas had murdered a child twenty years earlier, and although he'd been found not guilty—the child's broken neck and head injury were blamed on a fall from Phineas's hayloft—there were some in town who maintained that Phineas, a mysterious character who lived alone, was somehow responsible. A year after the child's death, Phineas further isolated himself, rarely coming to town. His house, choked by weeds, had started to look like a natural part of the earth itself, an overgrown hump of vines and moss, according to the few people who claimed to have seen it. Until the day he carried Mary to the doctor's front door, it had been two years since anyone had laid eyes on him. Many people had just assumed the old man had died, but no one had bothered to follow up on their conjecture.

Upon learning that Phineas T. Rider had saved his daughter's life, the sheriff said, "Whether that child died by his hand all those years ago or not, he's square with me. His debt's been paid." On other occasions, the sheriff said, "I never did believe he'd killed that child. You can't keep twenty-four watch over your own hayloft, now can you?" Weeks after the snake bite occurred, the sheriff said, "I should pay the old man a visit. To offer my thanks." But he never did.

Mary saw how easily it could happen—the accusation followed by isolation—because she had seen it happen to herself. She also saw how the old man's act of saving her was his way to set things right with the townsfolk. Her father called it redemption.

"Some men eventually redeem themselves. Others are incapable of it," he said. "Those are the ones we hang."

•

As her leg healed, she spent a good deal of time thinking about Phineas T. Rider. What did he do all day? What did his house really look like? Was there anyone—anyone at all—to whom he spoke regularly?

When she was ready to go back to school, she decided to look for Phineas's house on her walk through the woods. The few friends who had been with her the day of the snakebite no longer spoke to her, leaving her to walk through the woods alone, which was fine: they certainly wouldn't have understood Mary's fascination with a man who had been accused of murdering a child.

During that first week, as hard as she tried, she couldn't see anything that resembled a house. But then she had an idea. She waited until a cool night and then walked to the highest elevation in town, which she had already staked out, and from this vantage point she peered out over the woods looking for evidence of Phineas's house. And sure enough she found a thin twist of smoke deep in the woods. From the best she could determine, the house was located closer to the south part of the woods, where no path could be found. She would have to fight her way through weeds and fallen trees, risking more snakes and God only knew what else, but seeing where Phineas lived had become more than just idle curiosity; it had become a chance to glimpse her own future. *This could be me*, she mused.

•

The next morning, Mary set off to find the old man.

Before she could veer off the path toward where she believed Phineas lived, a group of boys and girls stood waiting for her by the fallen tree.

Andrew White was a fat boy, whose double chin waddled when he turned his head, and until this moment, Mary didn't even realize that Andrew had any friends. He stepped out from the whispering assembly and said, "Let's see it."

"Let's see *what*, Andrew?" Mary said. She grinned defiantly, expecting those who normally would have spoken ill of Andrew White to smile along with her, but all eyes remained on Andrew, who held some heretofore unseen power over her old friends.

"Let's see the mark on your leg," Andrew demanded. He was holding a Bible. Mary saw that now. Andrew's father was a minister with a tiny church in the deep woods, but Mary had never met anyone who worshipped there.

"We're going to be late for school," a girl behind Andrew complained. Mary had assumed the complaint was leveled at Andrew for making this silly request, but then the girl said, "Come on, Mary. We're not playing. Do what Andrew tells you to do."

Mary took a deep breath. Sensing the mood had shifted, Mary began to shiver. "Okay then," she said, and she hiked up her skirt to reveal the two still-crimson fang marks. The skin around the marks was as puffy as a snake's throat.

Andrew White moved closer to examine Mary's leg. The other children formed a circle around her, as though they'd rehearsed this moment. Andrew knelt down, set the Bible on the dirt, and took Mary's leg in both hands, the way he might hold a small, valuable statue. While on his knees, he peered up at Mary once, and she remembered dragging the long snake behind her, barely able to move her leg at all. A chill ran up through her.

Andrew picked up his Bible, stood, brushed off his knees, and walked backward, until he had reached the circle of Mary's former friends. He raised his Bible in the air and shook it while pointing to Mary's leg with his free hand.

"Behold!" he yelled. "The mark of the beast!"

Mary opened her mouth to laugh, but the other children reached into their satchels, removed various objects, and began throwing what they held at Mary. Mary didn't move at first, frozen in place as her head, torso, and legs were hit with old, hardened bread, a ball of twine, a piece of fruit. But then, as more things hit her, she screamed and crouched, yelling for them to stop.

"Satan lives among us!" Andrew called out.

Small pebbles, a pencil, and an apple core struck Mary. A clump of dirt exploded against her ear, causing her to tip over onto her side and clutch her head.

When Phineas T. Rider stepped out from the woods, the children scattered, all except for Andrew White. Andrew held the Bible up to Phineas and said, "Are you going to kill me, too?" He asked this without fear. It was more of a challenge, a dare, but Phineas ignored Andrew, scooping Mary off the ground and carrying her safely away, into the woods.

•

"You and me," Phineas said as he carried Mary, "we're the same."

Mary had her arms around Phineas's neck. She was shivering and sniffling.

"How did you know I needed help?" she asked.

"I din't," he said. "Two times you been where I walk. Same place."

"They said I had the mark of the beast," Mary said.

Phineas nodded. "They would."

Phineas reached a house that looked as she'd imagined it, like something out of a fairy tale: low to the ground and covered in vines and weeds. He carried her inside and set her on a bed that was no more than a board covered by a thin blanket. There was only one room, dark and cool, and it smelled smoky. Phineas lit two candles. He busied himself at the corner of the house, opening cabinet doors and then stirring something in a bowl. Mary thought he was making her something to eat, but when he returned, he nodded at her cuts.

In the bowl was paste, and Phineas used a wooden spoon to apply the paste to Mary.

"Use it my own self," Phineas said. "Look at me. As old as old gets."

Mary nodded. She showed him the places it hurt most—below her left ear, her right thigh, both elbows.

As Phineas smeared paste onto each place, Mary thought she could see a pair of eyes peering into the house from a window that wasn't entirely covered with vines.

"It's *him*!" Mary screamed. "It's Andrew come to get me!"

"You're safe with me," Phineas said.

But she wasn't safe with Phineas. She felt it in her chest.

Phineas finished applying paste to Mary's wounds and told her to get some rest.

"I need to go to school," Mary said.

Phineas said, "And who'll be waiting for you there?"

Mary could still see them, Andrew and her old friends, as though they were ghosts now surrounding her, their hands reaching into satchels, pulling out things to throw at her. She understood why her father hung the men he did, those incapable of redemption. She started to drift off as Phineas sat in a chair across the room and lit a pipe, the sweet smoke traveling toward Mary, wrapping around her like a silk cocoon.

•

Mary was asleep on the old man's bed when a distinct noise invaded her dreams: a hive of bees. The buzzing grew louder and louder, straddling both Mary's dream life and her waking life, and for a moment, as she opened her eyes and tried to focus, she was unsure where she was, whose unfamiliar bed she was in, or what was happening.

The room was lit with four candles now, but it must have been night for she could see flickering torches outside. Mary stumbled out of bed and ran to the window through which she had thought Andrew White was peering earlier. The buzz was a crowd of people outside Phineas's door, some young, some old, including her father, and the door to the shack was about to give way as someone outside attempted to cleave it open with an axe.

Phineas sat calmly in a chair, his eyes fixed on the door.

"What's happening?" Mary asked. Her hands were shaking. Wave after wave of shivers ran up through her.

"They think I've done evil," he said.

Mary, her voice strained, said, "What do you mean?"

Phineas shook his head, resigned. "It's coming to an end now."

Mary approached the door. She yelled, "Go away! Leave us alone!"

"There's no stopping an approaching storm," Phineas said. "I've seen it before."

Each time the axe hit the door, Mary screamed. It was as though the axe were meant for her. And maybe it *was* meant for her—all those things thrown at her earlier that day, pelted as she was by whatever her classmates could get their hands on. Maybe they'd gone to town to gather more people to dole out an even harsher punishment. She remembered his voice, high and shrill: *Behold! The mark of the beast!*

Mary collapsed to the floor as the door split in two. Several people kicked the broken door so that it opened down the middle. Two men pulled her from the old man's house even as she protested, screaming and punching, her heels collecting splinters along the floor.

"What are you *doing*?" she yelled. "Let me *go*!"

That's when she saw a noose hanging from the thick branch of a tree. Sitting in the tree was an older boy she recognized from school, a boy who had once killed a frog with the side of his fist. He had evidently climbed up there to tie the noose to the branch.

Mary was certain they were dragging her to the noose, so certain that she wailed and kicked, tears streaking her face. But then she saw her father lead Phineas T. Rider to the tree, along with two other men, and together they quickly bound his hands behind his back and his ankles together and then lifted him up into the air so that the older boy in the tree could place the noose around his neck. For a moment, Phineas looked as though he were floating up into the sky on his own, as though God were saving him from the hands of man. But then the boy in the tree tightened the noose around Phineas's neck.

"*No!*" Mary yelled. "He *saved* me!"

"Hush now," an older woman said to Mary. "The devil's speaking through you."

Mary spotted Andrew White in the distance, clutching his Bible in both hands, his lips moving in prayer.

Mary pointed at Andrew White and screamed, "It was *him*. He *attacked me*!"

Andrew White's parents, as fat and pasty as their son, stepped in front of Mary and said, "It's a sin to lie, girl."

"You're murderers!" Mary yelled. "Murderers!"

Because there was no platform for Phineas to stand on, no trapdoor to open beneath his feet, the men let him hang there for a few minutes as he choked, his eyes growing wider.

Finally, Mary's father wrapped his arms around the man's ankles, which dangled near her father's neck, and he yanked down as hard as he could. He did this a few more times, just to be sure that Phineas's neck had indeed snapped.

Fat Andrew White lifted his Bible into the air and said, "For if we live, we live to the Lord, and if we die, we die to the Lord. So then, whether we live or whether we die, we are the Lord's."

"I hate you!" Mary screamed. She broke away from whoever had been holding onto her and charged Andrew. Grabbing his doughy face, she tried sinking her fingers into his eyes. Andrew dropped his Bible, and a howl erupted from his mouth as Mary pressed harder, all the while pushing him backward toward a tree. Something had come apart inside her, and she was acutely aware, even as she was doing what she was doing, that her actions were wrong . . . and yet she couldn't stop. Andrew was helpless—weak, even—and Mary was confident beyond doubt that she could kill the boy.

It took three adults, all men, to pull Mary from Andrew as another man pried her fingers from the boy's eyes. When her fingers came free, she saw that Andrew White's eyes had been clenched shut but that he was crying. She kicked his Bible at him. While a man she didn't know kept his arms wrapped around her torso, her father lifted her legs and held them together to keep her from kicking.

"Get some rope," her father called out.

"You're going to hang me, too, aren't you?" she said. "Good! I want you to!"

"I should," her father said. "But not today. There's still some hope you can be redeemed."

"Is there?" she asked. The words came out of her mouth like venom from a fang.

"There is," his father said calmly. "There surely is."

It was all Mary could do not to spit in his face. She realized that this was her new self, the new Mary, and that, whatever line she had crossed, she could never go back now. She suddenly hated everyone in this vile town—the adults, her classmates, her own parents. They were all here to make her life miserable, every last one of them, even the babies yet to be born in this unholiest of places. They could all burn in Hell for eternity, as far as she was concerned. Every last one of them.

Part Two

After the incident with Phineas T. Rider—a topic her father refused to discuss—Mary wasn't allowed to return to school. Instead, an old woman named Olivia Purdy, who had been a schoolteacher for over thirty years, came to the house to teach Mary, ending each day with a reading from the Bible—this at the request of Mary's father.

Mary's mother, Bernadette—a tall, striking woman with black hair and eyes as blue as sapphires—often excused herself whenever Mrs. Purdy came over.

"Oh, take the air," Mrs. Purdy liked to say. "It's good for you."

"I think I will," Bernadette would reply, and if Mrs. Purdy wasn't looking, she'd smile and roll her eyes conspiratorially at Mary, an acknowledgment of the old woman's silliness. Mrs. Purdy was, in many ways, silly: she wore tiny glasses on the tip of her nose and enunciated each and every word—but she was also a kind woman, who did not think Mary was an evil girl for the things she had done. And Mrs. Purdy would surely have heard about Mary since the entire town had heard. Ten years old, and her fate had been sealed.

•

Four years came and went—four years during which her father had refused to mention the incident. One day, when Mary was fourteen, Olivia Purdy stopped mid lesson and said, "I'm not feeling well today, dear. I think we'll just end here."

There were many days that Olivia Purdy didn't feel well—she was never shy about documenting her various aches and pains—but she had never ended a lesson early.

"Are you all right?" Mary asked, reaching down and touching her fang marks, which she did whenever she was nervous. Which was often. The fang marks had never gone away. Several times each day, without realizing what she was doing, Mary would reach down and rub two fingers over the marks, the way another person might pinch the bridge of her nose or chew her nails.

"Don't worry about me now," Mrs. Purdy said. "Nothing a little rest won't take care of."

Mary hugged her goodbye and saw her to the door.

"I'll check on you later," Mary said.

Mrs. Purdy nodded then made her way uneasily down the front stoop, heading in the opposite direction from the main thoroughfare. The old woman lived on the outskirts of town in a house no larger than the front room where Mary took her lessons. Mary had been there only twice before, but she could still recall the smallness of the house and the smell of it, like damp dirt and rotting fruit.

After Mrs. Purdy left, Mary paced about, unsure what to do with herself. Then she became worried about Mrs. Purdy. It wasn't like her to leave mid lesson. What if something serious was wrong with her? She was old, and like a lot of old women Mary had known in her life, Mrs. Purdy was likely to die sooner than later. Mary reached down, about to touch the fang marks again, but caught herself this time. She needed, she realized, to find her mother. Her mother would know what to do.

Outside in the brisk air, Mary couldn't remember the last time she had walked alone while other children were in school, and she worried someone might scold her, grab her by the arm, and take her to her father, whose jail was in a nearby log cabin. She decided it would be best to walk with purpose, head up, long strides, nothing apologetic or meek in her demeanor. Walking past First Hide and Leather National Bank, Peabody's Dry Goods, and the post office, Mary casually glanced around to see if anyone noticed her, but no one gave her a suspicious look. In fact, no one seemed to recognize her. Was it all about how one carried oneself? Was that how one got what one wanted from this world? She continued on, past the feed store and the general store, past the house where Mrs. Kent made dresses while her husband, Mr. Kent, made hats, past the land office. That's when she finally spotted her mother.

Mary hesitated before approaching. Her mother was talking to Ephraim Flynn, the odd fellow who sold medicinal tonics and remedies from a cart he set up each day at the side of the road. What could her mother possibly need from him, this man who sold a bag of live insects to be worn around the neck? Her mother didn't have chicken pox, cholera, or consumption. She didn't suffer from whooping cough or convulsions. Mary wasn't sure what any of these maladies were, but she'd heard people mention them, sometimes whisper them, and she could tell by the speakers' expressions that none were good. Did her mother already know about Mrs. Purdy's illness, and was she describing the old woman's symptoms to Ephraim Flynn? But how would she have known this already?

Mary'd had a nightmare once about Ephraim Flynn. In it, Ephraim approached her with his bag of insects and lowered its string over her head, settling it against the back of her neck. As he backed away, the string tightened like a noose, choking Mary, and bugs crawled out from holes in the bag, their tiny legs and antennae touching her flesh. She screamed so loud in the dream that she woke herself up. Covered in sweat and breathing hard, she opened her eyes and swatted her arms and chest, trying to knock away the dozens of bugs that weren't there.

For a moment Mary considered the possibility that her mother was buying a potion for her or her father, but why? Neither was sick. This theory, however, dissolved when Mary saw her mother laughing at something Ephraim had said. When her mother placed the back of her hand against her mouth to hide the laugh, Mary knew with absolute certainty what was happening. She knew because she, too, had laughed that way once.

It had been after church a year ago when Ephraim's son Jeremiah sat next to her on the pew. He had a lazy eye into which Mary could read any number of things, and he had a thick swoop of hair that hung interestingly over his forehead. Throughout the sermon, he had looked over at her several times. One time, he pretended he was falling asleep, but then he opened his eyes wide and smiled at her. After church, as the congregation mingled outside, he walked right up to her and said, "The preacher looks like a toad," and Mary laughed—too loud. And then she raised the back of her hand up to her mouth, to shield her laughter so others wouldn't know. But what she really didn't want anyone to know was that she liked this boy. She liked him in a manner that she had never liked any other boy. Mary thought about him for weeks afterward and imagined all sorts of things she could never tell anyone. Some nights, thinking about him, Mary felt on fire. She'd wake in the middle of the night, tangled in her blankets, her arms wrapped so tightly that she'd be unable to move at first, until, after quite a struggle, she wriggled free.

But Ephraim Flynn? His *father*?

Her mother looked around after she laughed, as Mary would have done, and then she touched Ephraim's shoulder with her fingertips and backed away. Ephraim smiled, but it was furtive, and he quickly packed up his supposed cures into his pushcart. While Mary's mother headed in one direction, Ephraim proceeded in another.

Mary needed to talk to her mother about poor Mrs. Purdy, but she decided to follow Ephraim Flynn instead, although she couldn't have said precisely why. She stayed several yards behind him, surreptitiously glancing behind her, taking ten steps forward before stopping to assess her surroundings. She had to remind herself that the best way to remain invisible was to be visible, and so she held her head up and maintained a confident gait while still calculatedly lagging behind the peculiar man, who himself appeared to be on a dire mission.

Ephraim pushed his cart well beyond any of the public businesses, down streets where there were only boarding houses and horses tied to hitching posts. The further he pushed, the fewer boarding houses there were, until he reached a stretch of weedy land on which sat an old barn. There were not many old barns in these parts, since most of the buildings had been constructed in the last ten years when the city officially became a city, but there were, here and there, a few rickety buildings remaining from the first settlers, and this barn appeared to be one of them.

Ephraim pushed his cart into a patch of overgrown shrubs, as though he had done this many times before, and then he walked over to the barn and pulled open one of its large doors. The door creaked shut behind him.

Since no one else was around, Mary decided that now was a good time to be furtive, walking on the balls of her feet, creeping slowly toward the barn. Mary knew this wasn't where he lived because she had been to his house many times, trying to talk Jeremiah, Ephraim's son, into going to the hangings downtown. It was Jeremiah's mother, in fact, who had first spread the notion that Mary was an evil little girl for doing such a thing; it was Jeremiah's mother who mentioned Mary's name in the same breath with Satan's.

Mary crept around the corner of the barn, expecting her mother to appear any second from the direction she and Ephraim had just come. Deep down, she knew this was what would happen, because she knew what sorts of plans she'd have made with Jeremiah if she could have made plans with him. She knew she'd have made such plans because of how her temperature rose at night and because of the kinds of things she thought about, those things that would forever stay inside her head, lest someone use it as proof that she and Satan were indeed of the same mind.

Mary waited.

Sooner or later, she thought. Sooner or later her mother would come walking toward the barn, and all the puzzle's pieces would fit snugly together.

A good deal of time passed before the barn door opened. Mary crouched, expecting to see an impatient Ephraim Flynn, but it was her mother. She must have taken a short cut and arrived before Mary and Ephraim.

Mary's mother brushed off her dress, smoothing the wrinkles, while looking around for spectators, but there were none that she could see. Mary sunk even lower to the ground, but then a sudden fear of a snake biting her caused her to spring back up in plain sight. Fortunately, her mother was already on her way, walking quickly (too quickly, Mary thought) in a part of town where she had no business to be.

Mary made her way promptly to the street, hoping to escape before she was spotted, but when the barn door creaked open again, Ephraim

Flynn emerged whistling a tune. Mary froze. He didn't see her right away, as he was busy shutting the barn door and then adjusting his shirt.

While Ephraim walked toward his concealed pushcart, Mary thought she could make a run for it, but then he glanced up. A dark look crossed his face at the sight of Mary, as though he wanted to strike her. But then he smiled—a forced smile, Mary thought—and said, "Mary? Is that you?"

"Yes, sir," she said.

"What are you doing all the way out here?"

Mary said, "My teacher is ill. Mrs. Purdy? I was looking for her house to see how she's feeling."

Ephraim said, "Mrs. Purdy lives all the way on the other side of town. Don't you know that?"

"No, sir," Mary lied.

"How long have you been standing there?" Ephraim asked.

"Just long enough to notice your pushcart," Mary said. "I recognized it, and I thought maybe something terrible had happened to you, sir."

"Something terrible? Like what?" Ephraim Flynn smiled wider and took several steps toward her. Was he going to murder her?

Mary shrugged. "I don't know. It just didn't seem right. Your cart being there."

"I see," Ephraim said. "And did you notice anything else unusual while you were standing there?"

"No, sir," Mary said.

"Nothing at all?" Ephraim asked.

Mary shook her head. *Be calm*, she told herself. *Be calm*. "How's Jeremiah?" Mary asked.

"Jeremiah?" Ephraim repeated. His smile faded. "You're a smart girl, aren't you?"

"I hope he's well," Mary said. "But I really should go find Mrs. Purdy now."

"All right," Ephraim said. "You run along now. You go see how old Mrs. Purdy is doing." Mary took two steps when Ephraim said, "Wait! Here." He pulled his pushcart from the hedges and opened it up. He reached inside and pulled out a blue bottle. He shook it several times and said, "Give this to Mrs. Purdy. It's a tonic. A cure-all. Very effective." Mary reached for the bottle, but Ephraim quickly pulled it back, out of her reach. "But you'd better show this to your mother first. And tell her who gave it to you and where you found me. Tell her you saw me by this old barn and that I gave you this to give to Mrs. Purdy." He wasn't looking anywhere except into her eyes, as if staring at his own reflection inside them. "It's always best to make sure your parents know what you're doing. And that'll keep me from getting into trouble, too." He winked at Mary and then handed over the bottle. Rolling his pushcart away, he called out over his shoulder, "Just make sure she shakes it. Two small sips in the morning. Two small sips at night. And she'll be as good as new! Good day, Mary."

"Good day to you, Mr. Flynn."

•

Mary didn't give the bottle to her mother or to Mrs. Purdy. She dropped it onto somebody's yard when she didn't think anyone was looking.

By the time she reached her house, her mother was already there, as Mary suspected she would be.

"And where were *you*?" her mother asked, but she wasn't angry. More curious if anything.

"Mrs. Purdy was sick and went home. I thought I'd check on her but didn't know where she lives."

"You do, too, know where she lives," her mother said. "Remember? Over on Webster Street? The very last house at the very end of the block?"

Mary shook her head. "I don't feel good myself now."

"You should get some rest," her mother said.

Mary obeyed. In fact, she had wanted to go to bed so that she wouldn't have to face her father, who often said that he could peer into a suspect's eyes and determine what he was hiding. "I see things other men don't," he had said once when Mary had visited him at the jail, his feet up on his desk, ankles crossed. "That's why I'm the sheriff and not a deputy," he added, staring into her eyes.

No, it was better to steer clear of everyone until she could sift through all the various pieces. Not that nighttime brought any peace. She spent most of it awake thinking, and when she did slip into sleep, she dreamed of Ephraim Flynn and his dreadful bag of live insects. She kept slipping into and out of sleep, but each time it was the same dream—Ephraim placing the bag's string over Mary's head, as though helping her with a gruesome necklace. *Why can't I stop this dream?* she wondered once she had awoken, her chest quickly expanding and contracting. *What's happening to me?*

The next morning, Mrs. Purdy arrived at the usual time. Mary was so happy to see her that she wrapped her arms around Mrs. Purdy and pulled her close. The old woman was short, and since Mary was growing taller by the day, their heights had recently evened out.

"I was worried about you," Mary said, still holding onto Mrs. Purdy.

"Worried about *me*? You shouldn't do that, dear. Why, I survived the cholera epidemic when it swept through and killed an entire town. Not this town. Another town. That was before I moved here, dear. Before you were born. I survived scarlet fever and smallpox, too. You don't go worrying about me now, you hear?" She took Mary by the shoulders and stared at her. "But look at you! You look terrible."

"I couldn't sleep," Mary whispered.

Her mother walked into the room and said, "She came home sick yesterday. Said she went out looking for you." Then, cheerily, she said, "I believe I'll take a morning walk before the weather turns."

"Oh, yes, take the air," Mrs. Purdy said. "It's good for you."

Mary knew her mother was trying to get her attention so that she could roll her eyes, but Mary refused to look. On the one hand, Mary didn't want her mother to leave the house, because leaving the house meant that she would learn from Ephraim Flynn where Mary had been yesterday afternoon. On the other hand, if only to unburden herself of this knowledge, Mary wanted her mother to find out. Both choices, however, made Mary's stomach hurt, and she couldn't help grimacing.

"Oh, dear," Mrs. Purdy said. "Perhaps *you* need the day off today as I did yesterday." In a lowered voice, Mrs. Purdy asked, "Is it your time?"

"My time?" Mary asked, suddenly frightened. Time to *die*? When Mrs. Purdy glanced down in the general direction of Mary's waist, Mary understood what Mrs. Purdy meant.

"When I was your age," Mrs. Purdy said, "they called it 'female hysteria.'" She snorted at the thought.

"Oh," Mary said. Mary really didn't want to talk about this, but no other subject came to her, except for that *other* subject.

"You *do* know what I'm talking about, don't you? You're not a late bloomer, are you?"

"No, I know," Mary said. "It's not that."

"I have some black cohosh, if you want some," Mrs. Purdy said. "It helps my rheumatism."

Mary shook her head. She didn't know what black cohosh was, and she didn't want to know.

"I've been told," Mrs. Purdy said, "that *Cannabis indica* is also effective, although I've never personally tried it."

"That's not *it*," Mary said more forcefully than she intended. "That's *not* the problem."

Mrs. Purdy looked as though her feelings were hurt. "Well then," she said gently, opening her satchel, inside of which she kept her daily lessons. "I suppose we should begin."

"I'm sorry," Mary said, but Mrs. Purdy wouldn't look up. "Really," Mary said. "I am."

"I suppose we should talk about your reading assignment," Mrs. Purdy said. "Yes, let's start there."

•

Mary's mother, stepping through the door a few hours into the day's lessons, looked pale and weak. Even from a distance and with her bad eyesight, Mrs. Purdy remarked on how poorly Mary's mother looked.

"I do believe I've passed something on to Mary, and now Mary's passed it on to you," she said. "I suppose the next victim will be the sheriff."

At the mention of Mary's father, Mary and her mother looked at each other. *So*, Mary thought. *You know now.* There was no reversing time. It stood between them, Mary's knowledge of the evil deed. But then the light in the room shifted, as it often did at that time of the day, and Mary saw her mother differently. She saw a sad woman married to a man who never made her laugh, and Mary couldn't help thinking of the tree of knowledge, the way her father had told it from the serpent's perspective.

"I need to lie down, I think," her mother said.

"You do that," Mrs. Purdy said. "Some rest will do you good. It did me good yesterday, that's for sure."

Mary's mother nodded, although her thoughts were clearly across town, where the man with the bottled potions must have stood pining for this sad woman even as he wondered about his own fate. Everything that mattered in life, Mary thought as she watched her mother walk away, hung by the barest of threads.

•

That night, in her dream, the bugs tore through the canvas sack. In addition to all the ants, grasshoppers, and centipedes, there were wasps, too, and they sunk their stingers into Mary, one after the other, even as their wings brushed against her flesh.

Mary opened her eyes and gasped. There sat her mother on the side of her bed, her fingers gently pinching her, nails digging into her skin. Mary sat up, trying to catch her breath.

"I didn't want to startle you," her mother said.

"It was a dream," said Mary.

"A bad one?"

"It's the bag of bugs," she said, and looked up at her mother for a reaction. Her mother, who held a candle, looked away. This was how it had been earlier during dinner with her father—whenever Mary caught her mother's eye, her mother peered down at her plate.

"Look at me," Mary demanded.

Her mother looked. She'd been crying. Mary could see that now.

Her mother asked, "Are you going to tell him?"

"How do you know I haven't already?" Mary asked.

Her mother said, "We're all still alive."

Mary took a deep breath. She said, "No, I'm not going to tell him. But what about Mr. Flynn? Are you going to keep seeing him?"

"Shhhhhh," her mother said. "You must never mention his name, you hear me?"

"Well?" Mary asked.

Her mother shook her head. "I won't see him again. I promise, love." She said, "He's a good man, though. He knows a lot about the world. He knows where there's a spring that makes a person stay young forever."

"That's Satan talking," Mary said.

"Maybe so," her mother said. "But sometimes you want someone to talk to you. Anyone."

"Even if it's Satan?" Mary asked.

Her mother ignored this last question. Or maybe she was afraid to answer. She put her hand on Mary's cheek. "Good night," she said, then leaned forward and kissed Mary's damp forehead.

Part Three

Four years later, the War between the States had begun, and the city's population grew with newly arrived Southerners—families from Tennessee, in particular, settling in southern Illinois. "Too rocky to farm down there," these new arrivals told the locals, but it didn't take long for them to discover that farming wasn't any better on their new land. You had to go farther north for the good soil.

"Too many Paddies," her father complained one night at dinner. "I don't like it."

Mary asked, "What's wrong with the Irish?"

Her father gave her a sharp look, as though the question were a challenge. Mary was eighteen now, her prospects for marriage in town were low, and her father's patience with her was shorter as of late. "They're a dirty people," her father said, "if that answers your question." He sighed, shook his head. "Take old Ephraim Flynn. What's that man ever done to earn an honest living?"

The name Flynn caused Mary's heart to speed up. She imagined the bag of insects. She imagined her mother and Flynn in the old barn on the edge of town. Did her father know something from all those years ago? Her mother kept her eyes trained on her plate, idly pushing her food back and forth.

"How's that make him dirty?" Mary asked.

The blow came before Mary saw it. Instead of reaching up to touch her cheek, which her father had struck with the back of his hand, she reached down and touched the scars from the old fang marks. There was a time when her father rarely hit her, but lately it didn't take much to set him off.

"Too many Copperheads in this town," he said, as though he hadn't just struck his own daughter. Copperheads—Northern Democrats who opposed the war—had become his favorite topic of conversation. He said, "They don't want us to get involved in the war. Leave the South alone, they say. Fine. I understand the position. I can't say I entirely disagree with it, either. If someone has slaves, what business is it of mine? But these Copperheads, they're causing too much trouble around here lately. Too many deserters moving here. I heard one of them say he'd rather lie in the woods until moss grew over his back than help free slaves."

Mary thought she might scream the next time he said the word *copperheads*. It was the repetition of the word and the way her father said it that made it feel like someone gouging out her eyes, the way she had tried gouging out Andrew White's eyes all those years ago. This was all her father talked about. The war. The Copperheads. The deserters. The trouble they caused the town. He spoke about it nonstop, repeating himself every meal, as though he hadn't said the exact same thing using the same words the day before. He never listened anymore. Not that he had ever been a very good listener, but he didn't even make an effort now. He just talked and talked and talked, and whenever anyone else spoke up to interject a thought, he'd cut them off or talk over them.

Throughout all this, her mother stared down at her food, occasionally spearing a piece of pork or scooping boiled beans onto a fork but mostly shoving it from one side of her plate to the other. Both she and Mary had to be careful, though, not to make her father think they were sick. He had decided that the doctor couldn't be trusted anymore and had taken to bleeding them when they fell ill. Her mother had numerous white marks up and down her arm from where her father had cut her with a knife to let the poisonous blood flow out of her while keeping the humors, as her father called it, in balance.

"We should have left Africans in Africa," her father said. "When all's said and done, they've been a lot more trouble than they've been worth. Wouldn't you say so?"

"Yes," her mother answered absently.

Mary, whose face still stung from the blow, kept her eyes low.

•

Mary's only respite came when she allowed herself to think about Jeremiah Flynn. Rumor was that he was leaving town soon. The thought of him leaving filled her with irrational despair—irrational because she rarely thought about him anymore—that is, until she heard that he was leaving town. Perhaps she'd always had in the back of her mind a plan for the two of them to get married one day. And now the news of his pending departure had loosened this fantasy, causing it to bubble up to the front of her thoughts. Could that have been it?

The day after her father struck her, she ran into Jeremiah outside the Feed Store, knocking her shoulder against his arm, causing him to lose his footing. He'd had to plant his palm against the Feed Store's wall to keep from falling.

"Whoa!" he said, laughing. "What's your hurry?"

"No hurry," she said and smiled. "Just not paying attention." She wondered if he had ever found out about his father's secret. And then another thought came to her, that Jeremiah's father and her own mother had known each other as a man knew his wife. The very thought made her blush.

"Easy now," he said, taking her by the elbow. "Are you all right?"

"I'm fine," she said. "I hear you're leaving."

"I am," he said. "Going to Chicago to stake my claim!" He laughed nervously. "Or maybe just to get away from here."

Mary said, "It's not so bad here, is it?"

Jeremiah cocked his head the way a dog did when a sharp whistle sounded.

"All right," Mary said. "It's awful. It's the worst."

"I wouldn't say *that* necessarily," Jeremiah said.

"A hideous place," Mary said, enjoying herself, "where snakes bite little girls!"

Jeremiah narrowed his eyes at her, and Mary wasn't altogether convinced he wasn't going to say something mean to her, but then his eyes brightened and he said, "Where people gossip because they have no ambition!"

"Where fat little boys rule the roost!" Mary said.

"Where people can't wait to move away from!" Jeremiah said.

"Where small minds shrink to the size of peas!" Mary said.

"Where the most exciting place in town is the Feed Store!" Jeremiah said.

"Where men sell bags of insects to cure the whooping cough!" Mary said.

Jeremiah's smile disappeared.

"Oh no," Mary said, "I'm sorry."

"It's all right," Jeremiah said.

"You're mad now," Mary said.

Jeremiah shook his head. "Not at all. But I really do need to get going."

"Please don't go," Mary said. "Not yet."

"But I really do . . ."

"Hold on," Mary said. "Please. I said something stupid. If you leave right now, I'll never forgive myself." She was on the verge of crying. "Please don't tell him what I said."

Jeremiah said nothing at first, but then he shook his head and smiled. The smile suggested that his father was a sore subject. "Why would I do that?" he asked.

Without meaning to, Mary took hold of Jeremiah's arm and said, "I don't want to hurt his feelings."

"I would never tell him," Jeremiah said. "Trust me." He leaned toward her and said, "You really should leave this town, though. It's not good for a person. It's bad for the soul."

Nodding, Mary let go of Jeremiah's arm. She wondered why she had waited so long to talk to him this way. Playfully. Flirtatiously.

Jeremiah walked away, but when he reached the end of the sidewalk, he called out over his shoulder, "Come to Chicago!"

"I may do just that!" Mary replied.

Stepping off the sidewalk's lip and without turning around to look at her, Jeremiah lifted his arm and waved goodbye.

•

A week later and Jeremiah was gone, while Mary remained, like a widow. The town was unrecognizable with all the deserters and Confederate sympathizers pouring in. Men were always whispering lewd things to Mary when she walked by, men whom Mary had never before seen, or they'd lick their lips for her benefit and then spit and laugh. They knew she was the sheriff's daughter, and they knew the sheriff's position on the war. Who in town didn't know his position? It was all that came out of his mouth.

One night at dinner, her father started in on his favorite subject, the Copperheads, but with a new twist: Josiah Woods. Under the unusual name of Clingman, this man Josiah Woods traversed southern Illinois and terrorized the locals.

"And guess what?" her father said. "He's a Copperhead. No surprise there. No, sir."

Mary's mother, whose jaw appeared to clench, continued sawing at her food long after she had cut through it.

"Clingman?" Mary said. "Does he have a fake first name, too?"

"Just Clingman," her father said.

"What's he done?" Mary asked.

"You name it. Murders. Robberies. He's burned down two bridges."

To break the monotony of her father's endless monologues, Mary said, "I've been reading about medieval torture devices."

Her father laughed and shook his head. "Have you now!"

"What you need is a crocodile tube," Mary said.

"A crocodile tube?" her father said, laughing harder. "Tell me you're making this up."

"No, I swear," Mary said. "It's real. You put the criminal inside a tube, and the tube has these teeth that slowly press into the criminal so that he can't move. All you can see are his face and feet. And then you start a fire under the tube to heat it up."

"A tube?" her father asked. "How do you construct a tube that won't catch fire?"

"I don't know," Mary said, "but you can also inflict pain on the exposed parts. According to the book I read, facial mutilation and toe ripping were preferred choices."

"A tube," her father said. "I'm having a hard time imagining what it looks like."

"Okay then," Mary said. "How about a knee splitter?"

Her father's eyes lit up. "Now, I *do* know what a knee splitter is. Saw one once when I was a kid." He shivered. "Now *that* would hurt, by God."

"What we really need around here," Mary said, "is something called the brank."

"What's that?" her father asked.

"It's for women who gossip," she said. "It's a metal cage that goes over the gossiper's head. You hang all kinds of ridiculous ornaments on it to humiliate the woman. A bell is attached at the back of it to announce the arrival of the town gossip."

"I don't understand," her father said. "How does it hurt?"

Mary explained how most of them were designed simply to humiliate. "But there's one with spikes that penetrates the flesh when the gossiper speaks and . . ."

A scream so loud and tortured interrupted Mary, causing her to think a small animal was biting her mother beneath the table.

"What's wrong?" Mary asked, frightened. "Are you hurt?"

"Stop it!" she yelled. "Just stop it! The two of you speaking of torture. It's awful."

"We're only talking, Bernadette," her father said. "Get hold of yourself."

"No," her mother said. "You're not just talking. You're *savoring* it. You're *enjoying* yourselves."

Mary had wanted to defend herself, to say that it was better than listening one more time to her father's outrage over the Copperheads, but she let it go.

"I'm sorry," Mary said.

Her father said nothing. He dug back into his food. Soon, all three were eating in silence, their forks clicking against the plates, a pack of dogs barking somewhere nearby. But then her father said, "They say this Clingman fellow has a lot of charisma. They say other men are joining him." Her father sighed and said, "I don't know what's become of this republic. I surely don't."

•

One afternoon after visiting Mrs. Purdy, who was bedridden these days and dependent upon her former students' help, Mary saw her mother talking to a man named Dunphy. She didn't know much about Dunphy— she didn't even know if Dunphy was his first or last name—but what she *did* know was that he was the most vocal of the Copperheads, her father having mentioned his name more than once over dinner. When her mother laughed and then covered her mouth with the back of her hand, Mary felt so weak she thought she might fall to her knees.

Unlike the time with Ephraim, Mary didn't want to follow them. In fact, she didn't want to know more than she already knew.

•

Over the next week, Mary kept seeing her mother standing around talking to Dunphy where anyone could see them. Once, Mary watched her mother squeeze Dunphy's arm and then lean up on tiptoes to whisper into his ear. Mary quickly sized up her surroundings and determined that no fewer than a dozen others had probably seen this, too. And then a theory materialized: her mother was attempting to take her own life. Why else would she be so brazen? Why else would she flirt with the worst of the Copperheads, her father's sworn enemy, where so many others could see and report back to him?

Mary wasn't planning to do what she did next; it just happened. She yelled, "*Mom!*"

When her mother turned in Mary's direction, she was still smiling, but when she saw that it was her daughter calling out for her, the smile disappeared.

"Mary?" her mother said. She left Dunphy and quickly made her way toward Mary. "Mary?" she said again as she approached. By now Mary was crying, although she was trying not to. "Mary, what's the matter, dear?"

"I . . ." Mary began.

"What?"

"I need your help," Mary said, although for the life of her Mary couldn't think of what she could possibly need help with. "I can't do all this alone," she whined.

"Do what?" Her mother looked over her shoulder, toward where Dunphy had been standing, but he was gone now. "Come on," her mother said. "Let me get you home."

Mary wanted to hurt her mother for being so indiscreet, so common. How would her mother like it if Mary slept with one of her lover's sons? Mary had a mind to do it, too, just to spite her mother. She didn't know if Dunphy had a son, but Ephraim Flynn sure did. She wanted to force her mother to think about her own indiscretions, her own follies.

When her mother put her arm around Mary to help her, Mary looked over at her father, who stood hidden in the shadow of the Feed Store's side wall. From his vantage point, he could have seen everything unfold. He met Mary's eyes and then put his finger to his lips. *Shhhhh.*

•

Remarkably, it was an uneventful night at home, as were the two nights that followed. Her mother stayed in, and her father ate dinner without bringing up his favorite subject. If the ghost of what they all knew hadn't been lingering in the room, Mary might have been encouraged that they had returned to a time when things weren't so tense between the three of them, a time when Mary could eat her food without the fear of getting slapped for saying the wrong thing, a time when her mother still participated in the conversation. But had such a time ever really existed, Mary wondered, or was the threat of violence always there, coiled and ready to strike?

On the third morning after the incident, Mary's father opened her bedroom door and walked inside, as though it were the front door of their house, and he walked right up to Mary's bed and looked down at her. It was dark in her room, dawn just starting to break, and her father's features were murky, not fixed in place. When he spoke, his voice didn't match the movement of his mouth, which made Mary think the devil was speaking through him.

"There's going to be a hanging at one this afternoon," he said. "I want you to go around and tell people. I want you to get as many people as possible to come out."

"I haven't done that since I was a child," Mary said.

"You'll do this today," her father said. "This one's important."

"But . . ."

"Hush. Don't disobey your father. Now go back to sleep," he said before turning and leaving her room.

•

Mary couldn't sleep. She knew she had to do what her father told her to do. She knew that much. Since her father had already left for work by the time Mary had risen, there would be no more discussion on the matter. She looked around for her mother, but her mother was nowhere to be found, either.

"Mother?" she called out. "Mother, where are you?" Mary's breathing became shallow, and she could feel a throbbing at her neck. *Where's my mother?*

"Mother!" Mary shouted. "Mother!"

She wanted to push away the most horrifying thought she could imagine, but it kept coming back to her: her father slipping the noose over her mother's head, then pulling the knot up against her throat until it was snug. Her mother's punishment would be a warning to all the women in town as well as to the men who made fools of the town's husbands.

Mary wept as she prepared for her door to door visits . . . visits that had given life to the notion that Mary was an evil little girl and thus needed to be shunned.

The sun was up now, but it was raining outside—spitting, her father would have said—and the sky was rapidly darkening while black clouds moved in from the west. Normally, she liked these kinds of mornings, where daytime felt like night and where everyone, damp and sad, walked around looking sleepy. She couldn't have said why she liked them. Perhaps because no one else did? Because it was the kind of weather that sent people back inside, where Mary didn't have to look at those who had been so cruel to her over the years? Today, though, as the rain fell straight down and threatened to become heavier, Mary imagined each drop a punishment, a needle sticking her or a slap across the face. She left the house without her parasol. It was a crude parasol, anyway, covered with animal skins. The skins still had hair on them for protection from the rain. Some of the hair was fine, as though from a pig, while some of it was thick and white, probably from a goat. Mary had paid little attention to its patchwork construction when she was a child, but lately the mere thought of the parasol made her queasy.

Outside in the rain, Mary considered her options, but in the end she defied her father and visited only one house. She knocked and knocked until, finally, Ephraim Flynn opened the door.

"My father requires your presence by the jailhouse at one o'clock," Mary said.

Ephraim was holding a glass bottle in one hand and a cork in the other. His spectacles sat on the tip of his nose. He looked like an old man now, someone more likely to speak of grandchildren than woo her mother. "Mary?" he said. "Is that you? Mary Gant?"

"Yes," Mary said. "My father, the *sheriff*, requires your . . ."

"Yes, yes," Ephraim said, raising his hand with the cork. "But . . . *requires?* What does that mean?"

Mary said, "It means you need to be there, Mr. Flynn."

"All right then," Ephraim said. "I will. But . . ."

"I really need to leave now, sir. You need to hurry."

Ephraim nodded. "I trust your mother is well?" he asked just as Mary had turned around.

Mary hesitated. Was she well? She decided not to face him again.

"One o'clock, sir," she said.

"All right then," he replied.

•

Mary felt as she had the day she was to see her grandmother's body in a wooden coffin, knowing that later they would be lowering her into the ground and that she—Mary—would have to scoop dirt with a shovel and toss it over the box. Her father had explained to her the night before what was going to take place and what her role in it would be, and all night long and into the next morning, Mary's stomach roiled and gurgled. As she accompanied her parents to the undertaker's house, where her grandmother's body had been taken, she felt with each plodding step that she was dying. Grief and nervousness were like strychnine running through her veins, and all she wanted was to curl up somewhere and wait for Death to place his mouth against hers and suck the final breath from her lungs.

At ten minutes to one o'clock, no one was standing outside the jailhouse, save Mary. The rain fell harder, dropping straight down, as though buckets of water were being poured down onto her from on high.

At five minutes to one, Ephraim Flynn appeared. He, too, had come without an umbrella but he was wearing a stovepipe hat, like the president's, and when he saw Mary, he tipped his head ever so slightly toward her, probably fearful that the hat would fall from his head and land in a puddle if he leaned too far forward.

At one minute to one, the sheriff walked out of the jailhouse's side door. He climbed the steps of the gallows alone. He stared disconsolately out into the rain at the only two witnesses. Clearly, he had expected more people. Many more.

The gallows his pulpit, the sheriff yelled out to his meager congregation, "Wherefore they are no more twain, but one flesh! What therefore God hath joined together, let not man put asunder!"

At this, Dunphy was carried out of the jailhouse by two deputies. His ankles were bound, his wrists tied together behind his back, and his mouth stuffed so that he couldn't speak. Mary's mother followed the men, crying and pleading. Apparently, her father had taken her mother to the jail to bear witness.

"I'm begging you. Don't," she said. "Please. Don't."

Ephraim Flynn walked closer to the gallows, as though to be closer to Bernadette, but then stopped abruptly. He didn't, Mary figured, want to find himself in Dunphy's position, and to move any closer, where the sheriff could identify him, might raise questions. Why, after all, should Ephraim Flynn, salesman of homemade remedies, care about the sheriff's wife?

The deputies carried Dunphy up the gallows. Mary's mother tried to follow, but one of the deputies grabbed hold of her as another deputy put the noose around Dunphy's neck.

"Let me go, Jim," she screamed, swatting at the deputy. "Let me go *now!*"

Her mother's voice was unlike anything Mary had ever heard before. It reminded her of a dozen animals being slaughtered, or of a locomotive braking but unable to stop.

Mary was shivering violently now, and she felt more alone than she'd ever felt. She walked over to stand beside Ephraim, who looked down at her, his face pale, water from the brim of his hat pouring between them.

"Does he know?" Ephraim asked. "About me?"

"No," Mary said.

"Then why did you bring me here?"

Mary was crying now, barely able to speak. She looked up at Ephraim and said, "To save your life."

From the gallows, with the noose around Dunphy's neck, her father yelled out, "The heart is deceitful above all things, and desperately wicked!"

"Jeremiah," Ephraim said to himself.

"Your son?" Mary asked.

"No," Ephraim said. "Chapter 17, verse 9."

Her father pulled the lever, the trap door opened, and Dunphy dropped through, his swift descent abruptly halted once the rope went taut, his head leaning all the way to the right as his body swayed. Mary's mother screamed. The deputy let her go, and she ran up the gallows steps and, stopping at the edge of the trapdoor, fell to her knees. Dunphy's body swayed before her, twisting left then right, again and again.

Mary's father stared down at her mother for the time it took to breathe in deeply and exhale, and then he walked away, down the gallows stairs. Along with his deputies, the sheriff entered the side door of the jailhouse. The door shut after them, leaving the dead and the grieving alone.

Mary turned toward Ephraim, who himself looked about to weep. She put her arms around him, and together they stood in the rain until Mary released him and said, "Now go home. Go home and don't ever think of my mother again. Do you hear me?" Her voice was pleading, begging.

With a trembling lip, Ephraim nodded, but there was no fear in his eyes. He said, "I still love her. I always will." And it was while staring back at his blurry, stupid, rain-streaked face that looked like it had been punched that Mary wondered what there was for her in this world where men yelled lewd comments, where boys she loved moved far away, where her mother would so easily fall into the arms of other men, where her father struck her face as a reflex to the mere words she spoke. And here was this pathetic man, whose own head might as well have been full of a thousand humming insects.

"No," Mary said. "For your own sake. Don't." But there was no telling him otherwise, and Mary remembered the serpent sizing up Eve: *She's mine.* When would it all end, she wondered. What would it take? For once, her father was right. The heart *was* deceitful above all things. And wicked. Desperately, desperately wicked.

•

That night, alone in her room while her mother wept loudly in another part of the house, Mary took from her closet a burlap sack. The sack writhed and hissed, but it was not filled with insects, like one of Ephraim's home remedies. Inside was a timber rattlesnake. Using a stick, Mary had lured the snake into the sack after the rain had stopped.

She sat on the floor now before the sack. Was she the evil girl that people in town had once believed her to be? Almost two hundred years earlier, Mary would have been burned alive by her own neighbors and friends, but that did not mean that no punishment awaited her now. There would always be punishment for girls like Mary.

She loosened the cinched opening of the sack, and the snake slid angrily free, unrestrained now. Using only her hands, Mary pulled the snake back toward her so that it wouldn't slip under a door and into another part of the house, but when she pulled the snake back a second time, it struck her arm, sinking its fangs into her flesh.

Mary expected this response, same as she expected the war deserters to yell lewd things at her or her old friends to throw objects at her. She expected it the way she expected her mother to find comfort with men who were not her father and the way she expected her father to punish the men. She pulled the snake back again, and again it struck her. As the snake struck her for a fourth and then a fifth time, Mary felt the truth fill her veins and course through her—that there never had been a serpent in a tree and that whatever it was that women were made of, it wasn't the rib of man. She had never met a man who would have given so much of himself for a woman.

She reached for the rattlesnake again, but it escaped this time, slithering under the door. Mary was having difficulty breathing now, and her vision blurred. When she reached up to touch her face and felt nothing, she imagined herself in a town square, tied to a post. She shut her eyes and thought, *I will pay for my sins, whatever those sins are, if that's what the people desire.* She wanted nothing more than to be left alone. There was no white light awaiting her. She knew that much. But maybe it wasn't too late to save her mother. If it made everyone happy, they could anoint her with their torches, flames to flesh, and she would burn brighter than all the women who came before.

CATCH AND RELEASE

With the morning's sour breath still ripe in his mouth, Jason thought he could taste a certain cheese sandwich he'd eaten as a child, but the memory, like a dying bulb, flickered and then blinked out before he could remember what kind of sandwich it had been or where he'd eaten it. Lately, cryptic memories swam up to him through senses he normally paid little attention to, as when he touched the folded tablecloth at a garage sale last weekend and remembered standing in an aisle of fabrics with his mother at So-Fro while she examined a bolt with geometric designs, so bored he thought he might start crying at the sight of all the triangles and circles and squares, until he discovered the display of plastic eyes, the kind you'd find on a teddy bear, with black pupils that moved when you shook them. The eyes, sold by the hundreds, came in all sizes. When he asked his mother if she would buy him a box of extra-large eyes and she told him no, he wished something terrible would happen to her. His rage was often disproportionate to the moment, as was his love, but those days were all so long ago, the sudden memory of the white-hot anger he felt toward his mother both frightened and saddened him. His mother had been dead a dozen years now.

Jason knew that a blow to the head sometimes caused vivid but fleeting memories to come swirling back to a person, but he had suffered no such injury, only a vague lightheadedness that came with falling in love. Her name was Marie, and she lay in bed next to him, on her back, with her eyes shut. Jason resisted the urge to touch her, fearful of revealing his chief flaw as a boyfriend: the penchant to cling. If he could have his way, he would glue one of his palms to her flesh; he would trail her everywhere, be always on her heels—but he knew that this was an ugly way to behave, and it had driven away more than one girlfriend. What he saw as devotion often came across as pathetic desperation.

Marie had fallen asleep during *River of No Return*, a movie starring Robert Mitchum and Marilyn Monroe. During the filming, Monroe had nearly drowned. She'd worn waders to protect her costume, but when she slipped and fell into the river, the waders filled with water, pulling her under. Jason had paused the DVD to tell this trivia to Marie, only to realize, after he'd concluded the story, that she was already asleep. Now, through the barely open bedroom window, he heard feral cats rambling across the backyard, the whispers of high grass against their fur floating up to him. They were probably returning to the storage hut, one of them carrying today's fresh kill on its dry, sandpapery tongue—a mole, most likely, though possibly a field mouse. The small rodents sometimes showed up on Jason's stoop without their heads. The cats, barely hidden in the unmowed lawn, would watch him retrieve it. He suspected this pleased them: Jason discovering their grisly gift, even though the fresh corpse always went straight into a Ziplock baggie and then into a much larger Hefty trash bag full of litter and leaves. Four months ago, he had begun feeding one stray cat. Now he had six—two adults and four kittens. Half the cats were black, the other half tigers.

"What are you thinking?" Marie asked. The TV still glowed, though nothing was playing.

"You're awake," Jason said.

Marie nodded. She was spooky that way. You'd think she was sound asleep, but then she'd open her eyes and ask you a question. Jason was about to tell her what he was thinking, but Marie shut her eyes again, as if the conversation had already come to an end.

Jason knew why he loved her. It was a simple thing, really. He felt he'd known her his entire life, or at least since they were children, even though they'd met only six weeks ago. In the short time they'd been together, Jason had told her things about himself he had admitted to no one—like the time he had been so angry with his mother for not buying him a toy he had wanted, he took his father's .38 caliber handgun from the banker's box inside the broom closet and pointed it at her. He was only six and was probably imitating behavior he had seen on TV, but even now, all these years later, the thought of what he'd done caused his stomach to cramp up. What if the gun had been loaded? What if he had pulled the trigger? His father had come up behind him and quickly snatched the gun away, and Jason had been sent to his room for the night without dinner. After the incident, the gun had been moved to a more secure hiding place, and no one ever mentioned what had happened, but it was one of a handful of episodes that still weighed on Jason.

For reasons Jason was unable to pinpoint, he couldn't stop talking when he was around Marie. He'd never felt this way around anyone before, and it was a relief to unload some of the things he'd been carrying around since childhood.

Marie, on the other hand, remained silent, but it wasn't a judgmental silence. She was a vessel, taking in all that Jason had to offer. The things she told him in return were sparse and unambiguous: she preferred spring to fall; her favorite food was Italian; she needed a new car but couldn't afford one just now; she'd never been married and didn't want children.

"They're not for me," she had said, as though they had been talking about a style of shoe.

Marie opened her eyes again now, as eerily as before.

"I know you're thinking something," she said. "I can feel it." Staring at the ceiling, her gaze seemingly trained on a crack in the plaster that Jason had failed to notice until this very second, she said, "Tell me your secrets."

"I'm thinking about that missing dog. Have you seen the signs?"
She nodded.

Jason said, "I'd really like to look for her."

"Now?" Marie asked.

"If you don't mind," Jason said.

It was three in the morning by the time they left the house, each holding a flashlight. The dog's name was Molly, but they didn't call out for her. Instead, they listened for the jingle of a collar, looked for the suspect shadow behind hedges.

After an hour of creeping through strangers' yards, crouching to peer dog-level, Marie said, "We'll look again tomorrow."

Jason wanted to take hold of Marie and not let go. He'd never been this attracted to anyone he'd ever dated or longed for. The pull was gravitational. Unable to hold out any longer, Jason reached over and touched Marie's arm, revealing in one swift and impetuous gesture more than he'd meant to.

•

Jason was an assistant professor of history at the state university in southern Illinois near where he'd grown up, a part of the country he had tried but failed to escape from. His area of research was the Japanese internment camps during World War II—or, more specifically, the phenomenon of America's collective amnesia in the aftermath of a crime against humanity. For the six years of work toward his PhD, Jason had burrowed into his subject, interviewing over a dozen survivors—mostly men and women who had been children when their families were forced to move to a camp but also a few who had been young adults at the time.

Now in his sixth year at the university—his tenure year—Jason had failed to publish a book. In fact, he hadn't so much as unboxed his dissertation during his time at State, publishing only one essay in a scholarly journal and two book reviews. A pittance.

Though he went through the motions for his tenure review, allowing senior faculty to observe his classes and interview his students, Jason braced himself for the inevitable outcome—that he would be let go. Secretly, he hoped the department would deny him tenure. After all that he'd put himself through—two advanced degrees and a good tenure-track position at a research university—Jason wasn't sure that this was how he wanted to spend his life. To be denied tenure might just be the best possible outcome he could hope for.

At home, in his backyard, he sat in a lawn chair and watched the feral cats. He held a cup full of Purina Cat Chow and shook it, hoping to lure one of them over, but they remained at the entrance of the outbuilding, the adults and the kittens, unmoved by the bribe. When he spoke to them, they shut their eyes, as if the sound of his voice soothed them. Jason invested all his hope in their response, certain that one day the cats would come close enough for him to pet them.

"Look at you," Marie said. "Keeping a watchful eye on your brood."

Jason hadn't heard Marie's car, hadn't heard her footsteps. She was as quiet as the cats—quieter. In the short time they'd been together, they'd already fallen into a routine: Marie would show up after he came home from campus; they'd go for a walk together, searching for the lost dog; Jason would fix them something to eat while Marie napped; they'd make love as the food simmered; they'd eat; they'd watch TV; they'd fall asleep together on Jason's bed. At some point in the night, however, Marie would slip away, returning to her own apartment. He wasn't sure where she lived or what she did. When they had first met at a gallery during the city's annual Art Walk, she had said, "If we're going to make this relationship work, save any boring questions you have for another girl." He took her words to heart.

"You can stay all night, you know," Jason had told her more than once.

Each time, Marie nodded but didn't say anything. When he was younger, Jason might have described Marie to his friends as spooky, the sort of girl you were more likely to keep your distance from than date.

And yet now, as he and Marie took their daily walk together, Jason strategized on how to keep this odd, mysterious woman in his life.

"Look," she said. "A possum."

A dead possum lay in the road, its stiff fur moving to the ebb and flow of the breeze.

"You're running out of time," she whispered.

"Who?"

"You," she said.

"For what?"

"To domesticate the kittens," she said. "It's a small window before they turn feral for good."

"How long do you think?" he asked.

Marie shrugged. "A couple of weeks? A month?" She crouched and placed her palm on the body of the possum. "Still warm," she said.

•

Jason spent Friday morning on campus reading up on how to domesticate feral kittens. Marie was right: time *was* of the essence. Once a cat had crossed over, it would not only become difficult to domesticate, it might prove to be deadly to the cat, which was likely to run continuously in a panic or ram its head into doors or walls, trying to escape.

From his research, Jason also discovered that many cities, in an attempt to decrease the feral cat populations, had Catch and Release programs. A person could sign up for a humane trap designed to do no harm to the animal. Once trapped, the cat would be taken to the Catch and Release center where, along with dozens of other cats, it would be spayed or neutered by veterinarians who had donated their spare time to the cause. The cat would be given appropriate shots and, while still anesthetized, receive a light grooming. Later that day, the cat could be retrieved, kept in a safe place overnight, like a garage or basement, and then released the next morning or afternoon so that it could return to its colony. During his office hours, Jason made a few phone calls only to discover that no such program existed in his town or, for that matter, in any nearby town.

After wrapping up his Survey of 20th Century American History course, Jason decided to ask a student who volunteered at the local animal shelter if he could borrow one of the shelter's traps. Her name was Lucy, and she was disconcertingly covered from her neck on down with tattoos of vines and other foliage.

"I don't think I'm supposed to loan them out," she said, but then she smiled. In her bottom lip alone were three silver hoops. "Give me an A?" she asked. She was a senior, knocking out a general studies class that she should have taken two years ago, her last Gen Ed requirement.

Jason smiled and said, "We'll see."

They arranged to meet in the Barnes & Noble parking lot on Saturday morning, and Lucy, in a moment of uncharacteristic formality, offered an ivy-twined hand for Jason to shake. Although the sensation of her soft palm didn't match the gnarled and vine-laced flesh, something about the incongruity of what he saw as opposed to how it felt was strangely familiar to him. He couldn't place the memory, but a feeling of melancholy came over him that was so intense, it disturbed him.

"Good enough," Jason said, nodding, turning away.

•

Jason had first met Marie at Art Walk when the two of them were standing together and studying a modern-day take on the famous Dogs Playing Poker paintings. In this version, the dogs were sitting side by side at a bar, playing video poker.

"Jesus, that's depressing," Jason had said, and when he turned to Marie, he saw that she was crying. He was about to speak when Marie turned to him and said, "If we're going to make this relationship work, please save any boring questions you have for another girl."

The cafeteria where they ended up after visiting five more galleries together was the last of its kind in town, offering meat loaf for dinner, vegetables ladled up from silver tubs by old women wearing hairnets, and lime Jell-O desserts with dollops of whipped cream on top—an entire meal for less than five dollars. The building that housed the cafeteria was slated to be demolished in two months, at the end of the fall semester, to make way for a new 24-hour fitness center. When Marie tried to pay for her food with a credit card, the cashier, who may well have been ninety, pointed to the Cash Only sign.

Jason found it charming that the place had refused to budge out of the 1950s, let alone into the twenty-first century, but he also knew that this was likely the reason for its demise. Modernize or die, he thought.

Marie said, "Well, then. I guess I need to return it."

Jason stepped up and offered to pay for her meal, but the only way Marie would accept his generosity was if he gave her his address.

"I don't like to owe anyone anything," she said. "And I'd like to keep it that way."

"Fair enough," Jason said, and in a rare moment of confidence, he added his phone number below his address.

Jason marveled at the randomness of their meeting. He imagined a time in their future—five, ten years from now—when he could tell this story to their friends in a way that might sound apocryphal, like the 1959 meeting of Marilyn Monroe and Nikita Khrushchev, about which Marilyn had said, "Khrushchev looked at me the way a man looks at a woman."

On their dusk-lit search for the lost dog, Jason and Marie passed the dead possum again, but this time they didn't stop.

"Civilized cities pick up dead animals," Marie said. "They don't just leave them rotting on the road."

"Key word," Jason said. "*Civilized*." He turned to Marie, hoping to catch her smiling at him, but her eyes were wet and her nose was starting to run. "I'll call the city," Jason said. "On Monday."

After it had gotten dark, they sat in lawn chairs inside the circle of light from the streetlamp and watched the ferals.

"They're coming closer," Jason said. "Look."

The kittens shortened their distance between the outbuildings and where Jason sat by half, while the bigger cats hung back, fastidiously licking their front paws. The kittens sat and stretched in the grass but refused to come any closer. Jason shook the cup of food again, trying to entice them, but Marie took hold of his wrist and made him stop.

"That's as close as they want to come," she said. "Be happy." She turned to him and forced a smile, and something about the way the streetlamp lit up her face, along with her expression, convinced Jason that he had in fact once known her, but he still couldn't place when or where, and he was too afraid to ask.

Jason leaned forward and shook the cup again.

•

It had come to Jason in the middle of the night. Lori Jenkins. That's who Marie was—who she really was: the once-missing girl, now a woman, from his childhood. The girl from the telephone pole flyers. The girl everyone thought had died but had come back. The miracle girl.

That was twenty-five years ago, but it was her. It was Lori. She had changed her name to Marie. She lay beside him now, asleep, remaining in his bed longer than she had ever stayed since they'd begun seeing each other. He wondered what other secrets were inside her head. He wondered what a person who carried with her such a profoundly disturbing past was capable of.

Jason tried falling back to sleep, but it wasn't until an hour before his cell phone's alarm clock was to begin chirping that he finally drifted off. When he woke up an hour later, Marie was gone. It was as though a symbiotic relationship existed between Jason's state of unconsciousness and Marie's ability to flee, and in order for one to wax, the other needed to wane.

•

There wasn't much information about Lori Jenkins's abduction on the internet—nothing, at least, that he didn't already know. It had happened before Amber Alerts went into effect, before the national media became obsessed with missing children to boost their ratings. Furthermore, it had happened in southern Illinois, a part of the country few people cared about.

Jason searched for information about abductions, and what he learned was that girls Marie's age—the age she had been when she had been kidnapped—were three times more likely than boys to be victims and that the captor was almost always a man with a history of sexual misconduct, violence, and substance abuse. Not surprisingly, the main reason for abduction was sex.

Lucy was already in the parking lot now, sitting in an old hatchback and sipping from a thermos. Her car was plastered with a few dozen bumper stickers, all with a left-wing bent, a few radically so; and when Lucy stepped out of the car wearing a tank-top that revealed even more tattooed leaves and prickly vines, Jason wondered what it was about Lucy—what dark compulsion—that kept her from letting something simply be.

Earlier, Marie had texted to say that she would go with him to Barnes & Noble to pick up the trap from Lucy. For reasons Jason couldn't put his finger on, he really wanted to go alone but couldn't think of a pretext for asking Marie not to join him; but when Marie witnessed Lucy walking toward them in all her tattooed glory, Jason knew why he'd felt as he had. "Well, hel-*looooo*, professor!" Marie said to Jason before they stepped out of Jason's car.

"Lucy?" Jason said. "This is Marie. Marie Lucy."

Lucy smiled at Marie, then glanced toward Jason, as if to say, *So this is who you're having sex with.* He could tell that something curious pulsed behind her eyes by the extra deep breath she took and the way her eyebrows were raised. She walked around to the rear of the car and popped the hatch.

"Here it is," she said. "I'll need it back by Monday, though. I didn't tell anyone I took it."

"Will do," Jason said. "I appreciate it."

Lucy gave Marie one last once-over before getting into her car and driving away.

On their way home, Marie said, "She was disappointed you weren't alone."

Jason laughed.

"What I mean," Marie said, "is that she probably thought she was special because you'd asked her for a favor."

"Okay," Jason said, smiling.

Marie said, "Don't patronize me."

"Don't *what?*" Jason asked. He couldn't help it—he laughed again. "I'm not. I swear."

"Let me out," Marie said.

"Are you kidding me?"

"No," Marie said. "Let me out or I'll scream."

Jason pulled over to the side of the road. Marie opened the door and got out. She walked ahead of the car without looking back. Jason sat there, unable to think of what to say or do. He finally leaned over and shut the door, then drove away, passing her without slowing down. In moments like these, when he knew that pleading would result in a deeper retreat, he felt himself trying to stay afloat but being pulled under no matter what he did, whether he fought or relaxed.

"Goddamn it," Jason said and hit the steering wheel with his palm. "Christ," he said. "Christ Almighty."

•

Last week, Jason had stocked up on a variety of Chef Boyardee and Franco-American canned foods for lunches, if only because the sight of their labels brought to mind summer nights in childhood when trucks crept up and down side streets misting the air with insecticide or Sunday afternoons when there was nothing to do but watch black-and-white movies or World Wide Wrestling.

Back home with the humane trap, alone, Jason heated up a can of ravioli, stirring the pot like a witch in *Macbeth*. Along with the old familiar smell rose up images of childhood. Beginning in the fifth grade, Jason started seeing Lori Jenkins flyers around town, everywhere. The photo on the flier was a head shot of a nine-year-old girl with windswept hair—a photo chosen, he suspected, so that everyone could get a good look at her face. Above her photo was one word: MISSING. She lived two towns over from Jason, and she had been abducted, according to the flier, on the same day as his tenth birthday. The flier hung in the window of every store in town, on the bulletin board of Safeway's breezeway between the two sets of automatic doors, and on at least one telephone pole for every block.

Jason fell in love with Lori Jenkins that year, as he'd fallen in love with so many other girls when he was ten, but his love for her was more profound as he imagined being the one who found her walking with a stranger. He imagined how she would give him a look that said "Help me" or "I'm not supposed to be with this person," and he imagined wrestling her away from danger. He would free her. And because he had saved her, she would fall in love with him in return.

Over the two years that she had been missing, the flyers remained up, although the ones in the storefront windows turned yellow from the sun, and the ink on the ones on the telephone poles blurred from the rain and snow. The flier on the Safeway bulletin board stayed intact but would get covered over with fliers for used boats or guitar lessons, until someone—Jason never knew who—repositioned Lori's flier, returning it front and center. At the end of two years, the flier was a constellation of holes.

Jason eventually came to believe, like so many others, that Lori would never be found or, if she was found, she wouldn't be alive; but one afternoon in the fall, when all the town's children were in school, a girl was discovered standing in the middle of a busy intersection. She was wearing a sheer pink nightgown, no shoes or socks, and her fingernails and toenails were all painted the same shade of red as her lipstick. It was Lori Jenkins. She was eleven years old, and she was alive.

"A miracle," Jason's homeroom teacher, Mrs. Hammond, said the next day. "Like Jesus resurrected."

•

Marie returned as Jason was busy fixing the trap. He had spooned out canned tuna onto a paper plate and set it behind the raised piece of sheet metal that was to trigger the cage to shut as soon as a cat stepped on it.

"I don't want to talk about it," Marie said.

"Okay," Jason said, pulling the lever that set the trap. "We won't."

Marie sat down next to him and said, "Are they coming closer?"

Jason shook his head. "I sense a setback," he said.

"Be patient," Marie said.

Jason nodded, but he wasn't sure he had ever been that patient. His neediness was like an addiction that needed feeding. For Marie's sake, he nodded. He resisted the urge to pick up the cup of food and shake it; but the entire time he remained there, it was the only thing he could think about, and it took all his willpower not to do it.

•

On Sunday, the cats were nowhere to be seen. The trap was empty. Jason's heart sped up at what he feared—that the cats had crossed over to the other side and that no matter what Jason did or what he offered them now, they would never cross back. The window for domesticating them had slammed shut.

Marie drove over to console him.

"Let's go for a walk," she said.

The first few minutes of the walk were spent in silence. Neither mentioned the cats or even the missing dog. Jason knew that Marie was comfortable without words, but Jason wasn't. Even in class, whenever Jason asked his students a question, he couldn't bear the silence for longer than a few seconds before he offered an answer, even though he knew that he was supposed to let the silence linger until someone finally, mercifully spoke up. The one time he forced himself to remain silent in class, Lucy had stared at him with great sympathy, the way a person looks at someone who has lost a beloved pet.

"I did everything by the book," Jason told Marie.

Marie said, "You should never think that intellect is superior to instinct. Instinct will always win."

Marie was only making an observation, but the way she put it made Jason feel defensive. Would she have said that to him if he wasn't a professor? Was it a slight against his academic background, about which he had his own misgivings?

Marie paused at the site of the dead possum. The possum had been run over so many times, it was nothing but fur and concrete now. Someone who had not been tracking the dead animal's decay would have had no idea what they were looking at. It looked as though the road itself had begun to sprout a patch of fur.

The sight of the unidentifiable possum brought to mind all those times Jason rode his bike in grade school past dead animals, so many dead animals that he became immune to the sight of them—unless it was a dog or a cat, in which case he would stop his bike, get off, and check for a collar. If there was a collar and a tag identifying the owner, he would find the owner's house and, like a miniature soldier during wartime, deliver the unfortunate news of the death to the person who answered the door. Often, the response was anger or disbelief. Sometimes, it would be laughter, as though his presence were part of a larger gag orchestrated by friends. Occasionally, the response was hysteria, and Jason would watch as his existence to the bereaved disappeared entirely in the face of grief. More than one grade school teacher had told his mother that he tried too hard.

"He needs to temper his desires," Mrs. Hammond had told his mother during a parent-teacher conference, and his mother had reported this news afterward without any elaboration, the way another parent might have said, "Do your homework on time."

"I'm calling the city tomorrow," Marie said now.

Jason said, "I'm not really sure what they can do at this point."

"It's not what they can do," Marie said. "It's what they should have done."

Two blocks in the distance, Jason thought he saw one of the black ferals crossing the street, but he decided not to mention it to Marie, who was busy taking photos of the possum, using her foot to provide scale for someone who might desire perspective.

•

When Jason was eleven, his mother sat across from him while he ate a pimento cheese sandwich that she had made for him. He enjoyed repeating the word pimento over and over until it sounded like the strangest word that had ever existed. The more he said it, the more devoid of meaning the word became. "Pimento!" he would say. "Pimento! Pimento!" But on that day, he was unnerved by his mother silently watching him, so he ate his sandwich slowly, trying not to finish it in two or three large bites, as was his way.

"I found this hidden inside a magazine in your room," his mother finally said, revealing a folded sheet of paper. He knew before she opened it what she was holding: a flier for Lori Jenkins. But it wasn't just a flier of her. He had pasted a photo of himself next to her photo, and he had drawn hearts around the two heads. He had also drawn bodies onto the two heads, but the bodies were not wearing any clothes.

Jason stared down at the sandwich in his hands, which could have been someone else's hands holding someone else's sandwich. Then he stared beyond them to the tablecloth with the geometric designs, and he tried to lose himself in the various triangles and circles and squares, but the designs only reminded him of other vague memories of impatience and boredom. He tasted cheese and acid at the back of his throat.

"This isn't healthy," his mother said. "This poor girl. This poor, poor girl. Her parents are worried to death, and you're . . . I don't even *know* what you're doing. It's not right, though."

Jason nodded. He knew, even as he defamed the flier, that what he was doing wasn't right, but it made him happy to think about the two of them together; and absent the actual Lori Jenkins herself, the flier was the closest thing he had to being with this girl he loved.

His mother tore up the flier and stuffed it in the garbage. When she was done, she said, "I won't tell your father." She paused. She stared at him, as though he were a stranger. "This time," she warned.

The next day, Jason found another flier of Lori on a telephone pole, one of the newer flyers that hadn't yet begun to suffer from the elements. He removed it, folded it, and tucked it away. At home, he lifted from his parents' room a framed photo of himself from the third grade. He detached the backing, pressed the folded flier against the back of the glossy eight-by-ten, and then refastened the backing. He returned the frame exactly as he had found it.

It wasn't until his mother had died and his father had moved a thousand miles away that Jason, going through the things his father had left behind, remembered what was hidden inside the frame; and when he removed it and unfolded it, the sight of Lori Jenkins resurrected a host of complicated feelings that he had thought long vanished from his life— namely, what it was like to fall in love with the specter of a person instead of the person herself.

•

That night, in bed in the dark, when Marie opened her eyes and said, "I know you're thinking something," Jason replied, "I am."

"Tell me," Marie said.

"I wonder where all the missing dogs go," Jason said. "The ones that survive. I'm sure some are taken in by strangers, but others probably roam in packs. When I first moved into the house, there was a note under a rock at the end of my driveway. It said, 'Beware. A pack of dogs is loose.' That's all it said. I looked up and saw that everyone on the street also had a note pinned to the ground with a rock. Imagine. Someone had taken the time to do that."

"Did you ever see the pack of dogs?" Marie asked.

"I didn't," Jason said. "No." He paused before pushing on. "When I was a child," he said, "I fell in love with a girl I had never met."

"A lot of boys do," Marie said. "They fall in love with women they see on TV shows."

"It wasn't like that," Jason said. He wasn't sure if he should continue, but he was afraid if he stopped now, she would become angry with him. He said, "She was a missing girl. Her flier was everywhere." He took a deep breath and held it. He listened for a response from Marie, but there was none. He said, "Her name was Lori Jenkins, and she'd been abducted. For two years, I stared at her flier and wondered what she was like. I wondered if she was still alive." Jason wanted to impress upon her the depth of his love for this girl whom he had never met, so he said, "I wanted to be the one who found her. I wanted to be her hero."

"I see," Marie said.

"Do you?" he asked. "Because it doesn't put me in a good light. I think the other children thought I was—what's the best word?—peculiar. Do you think I'm peculiar?" he asked.

"Not at all," Marie said.

"Really?" He was relieved to hear her say this.

Marie said, "I think you're like everyone else."

"Oh," he said. "Okay then."

"I don't mean that in a bad way," Marie said. "Most people aren't unique."

Jason turned onto his side so that his back faced her. He brought his knees closer to his chest and tucked his arm under his head.

"Don't be that way," Marie said, but Jason couldn't help himself. He knew that he was sulking, and his behavior embarrassed him, but he couldn't help it. He offered up his emotions the way a child might.

"I'm tired," he said, finally. "That's all."

For the first time, Marie spooned behind him, holding him tight, but when Jason awoke only a few hours later, she was already gone.

•

In the morning, Jason sent Marie a text to apologize, but he received an autoreply that his message couldn't be delivered. He called her, but all his calls went straight to voice mail. He never knew where she lived, so going to her place wasn't an option, and he didn't know where she worked. He sat at his kitchen table, stirring his coffee, thinking how, after all these years, he had found the missing girl. But now that she had disappeared, he knew he would never find her again. It was a statistical improbability.

Fall bled into winter and then into spring. To Jason's surprise, he was granted tenure. A colleague came by his office to shake his hand and said, "I guess this is it then. I guess this is where you'll die." He said it jokingly, but Jason felt ill at the thought. The next year, Jason was on committees to recommend or deny tenure to his junior colleagues, and he envied their freedom, ever-diminishing though it was. "Leave before it's too late," he wanted to warn them.

A year had come and gone without a word from Marie. As he had predicted, she was gone forever. That fall, he and Lucy were living together. She was no longer a student, having graduated the previous May. He knew what his colleagues would think if they ever found out, but it wasn't like that. She was renting a spare room from him while she figured out her next move. It was a good arrangement for both of them. They were room-mates, even though she was younger than him by a dozen years, had more energy, more interests, and often talked about celebrities and cultural phe-nomena he didn't know. But she had never seen a Marilyn Monroe movie, and she did not know who Nikita Khrushchev was. He had told her the story of their unlikely meeting, but he left out what Marilyn, who had found the Soviet premier repugnant, had said to her maid afterward: "He squeezed my hand so long and hard that I thought he would break it. I guess it was better than having to kiss him, though."

On the night of the first snowfall of the season, they stood together in the backyard. She had removed her lip rings. Her winter coat and gloves covered the inked skin. In this light and under these circum-stances, she looked unlike anyone he had ever met. He imagined she was someone from his future, someone he would meet and fall in love with one day. A feral cat—perhaps one of the ferals he had hoped to lure to him last year—had given birth to five kittens, and the kittens were in the old storage hut next to their mother. They occasionally made mewing sounds—squeaks, mostly—but their eyes were still sealed shut.

Lucy took a flier from her pocket and said, "I found this in the

THE FEAR OF EVERYTHING

house." As she unfolded it. Jason expected it to be a flier for Lori Jenkins. He still had one tucked away behind his third grade photo, but how could Lucy have found it? When she handed it over, Jason realized that it was the flier for the missing dog.

"Did they ever find it?" Lucy asked.

Jason shook his head.

"Poor fella," Lucy said. She took his hand in her gloved hand and said, "You must be cold."

"A little," Jason said.

Lucy said, "We'll have better luck catching these ones. I have cat-catching skills heretofore unseen in this backyard." She smiled up at him. She often spoke using formal diction in an ironic way. It was one of the things Jason liked about her.

Beyond the hut, three backyards down from his, stood a woman he thought might have been Marie—something about her posture suggested so—but when the woman turned to face Jason, he saw that it was the new neighbor. He remembered now seeing a moving truck the night before while on his walk, its front tire parked over where the possum had once been. They had a dog, too, a big old St. Bernard, and Jason hoped that if he ever appeared on his new neighbor's doorstep, he would be bringing good news in the form of a happy dog that had only gotten loose. Jason waved, and the neighbor returned the gesture. Lucy, whose view of the neighbor was obstructed by the hut, said, "They'll wave back when their eyes open. Until then—patience, my dear man. Patience."